1

DIABOLIQUE

A Sibyl Novella

Marlene Pardo Pellicer

DIABOLIQUE: A SIBYL NOVELLA. Copyright © Marlene Pardo Pellicer. First Printing 2019. Printed in the United States of America

First Edition:
First Printing

PUBLISHED BY ELEVENTH HOUR LLC
www.11thhour.company

E-BOOK ISBN 978-0-9991605-8-9
PRINT ISBN 978-0-9991605-9-6

I dedicate this book to my ten writing companions:

Qui Qui, Elvi, Slim, Dot, Stripe, Onyx, Trouble, Coco, Djinn Djinn and Bubba.
They patiently lie at my feet while I write, listen to my every word when I read a
passage out loud to them, and only love and approval shines from their eyes no matter
how awful the idea... all in exchange for doggie treats.

Special thanks to Brandon Calvet for his idea on the Sempiterno Apostasy and the
Dispossessed

About The Author

Marlene has been in love with writing since she was eleven years old; but as they say, better late than never.

She is a native Miamian and the founder of *Miami Ghost Chronicles*. She has been a paranormal researcher since the 1990s and is the producer, host and narrator of *Stories of the Supernatural, Nightshade Diary, Supernatural StoryTime* and the blog author of *Stranger Than Fiction Stories*.

Marlene lives with her husband Henry on a micro-farm and bee sanctuary in Miami's 100-year-old agricultural belt, surrounded by several dogs (AKA writing companions), various exotic birds, a large flock of free-range chickens and a rescue rabbit named Thelma.

www.MarlenePardo.com

Other Books by Marlene

FICTION
Walker Between the Worlds: Book 1 of the Sibyl Novella (2019)

NON-FICTION
Haunted History of the Old West's Wicked Ladies & The Bad Hombres They Loved (2017)
The Lady in the Blue Kimono: Film Noir Murders (2018)
Supernatural Safety: A Paranormal DIY Guide (2018)

CHAPTER IV. THE MARRIAGE OF QUASIMODO

We have just said that Quasimodo disappeared from Notre-Dame on the day of the gypsy's and of the archdeacon's death. He was not seen again, in fact; no one knew what had become of him. During the night, which followed the execution of la Esmeralda, the night men had detached her body from the gibbet, and had carried it, according to custom, to the cellar of Montfaucon. About eighteen months or two years after the events which terminate this story... when a search was made in that cavern for the body of Olivier le Daim, they found among all those hideous carcasses two skeletons, one of which held the other in its embrace. One of these skeletons, which was that of a woman, still had a few strips of a garment which had once been white, and around her neck was to be seen a string of adrézarach beads with a little silk bag ornamented with green glass... The other, which held this one in a close embrace, was the skeleton of a man. It was noticed that his spinal column was crooked, his head seated on his shoulder blades, and that one leg was shorter than the other. Moreover, there was no fracture of the vertebrae at the nape of the neck, and it was evident that he had not been hanged. Hence, the man to whom it had belonged had come thither and had died there. When they tried to detach the skeleton which he held in his embrace, he fell to dust.

- Notre-Dame de Paris
Victor Hugo

They are neither brute nor humans-
They are neither man nor woman-
They are Ghouls

-The Bells
Edgar Allan Poe

Contents

1. The Stowaway

The *aviso* ship, *San Amaro*, cut through the blue waters of the Gulf of Mexico as a steady wind filled her sails. The courier vessel, though well armed, could outrun larger, better-armed boats. In its hold, it carried something that could prove more valuable than goods or gold. Correspondence to and from the Spanish throne and its holdings in the New World became the most sought after prize of spies. Among lists, tallies and letters to loved ones, secret missives held information that could bring down an empire. On this occasion, it carried two passengers when it sailed from La Coruña, Spain on November 3, 1798.

A woman stood at the railing of the main deck, a breeze moved a thin black veil covering her face. Dressed in a deep purple gown with a black overdress and ebony gloves, her outfit proclaimed she mourned for a family member.

The captain came to stand next to the mysterious figure. His troubled eyes glanced at the pale, impassive face behind the mantilla. He kept his voice low as he said, "I've lost another one."

They both understood he referred to one of the crew.

"When will we arrive in New Orleans?" Her voice remained steady.

"Tonight and we can disembark tomorrow morning."

"This will be a dangerous night. If you can row me to shore when you drop anchor, it will follow me."

"How can it?"

"It has ways. The longer it remains on board, the more danger there is for your crew."

"And the monk?" The captain's eyes shifted to a figure on the other side of the deck.

"He can go with you when you go ashore in the morning. Leave my belongings at the convent with the Ursuline sisters."

"As you wish, but I fear for you." He stated with heartfelt regret.

"Captain Fermin, I appreciate your concern, but the quicker I get to land the safer it will be for everyone, including myself."

The man's eyes filled with doubt, as he tried to discern if the woman who stood before him experienced any fear. Her voice did not quaver, and the glint of her green eyes reflected a courage he doubted he could muster when confronting whatever stalked the humans on this craft.

Her next words confirmed the trepidation lurking in his heart. "Captain, make sure the sailor you choose to go with me brings a religious artifact he can carry on his person, and if it's made of iron the better."

He nodded to her and strode off in the direction of his quarters.

DIABOLIQUE
A Sibyl Novella

Ema closed her eyes and willed away the desperation enveloping her. Physical exhaustion washed over her; confined to a ship for so many days, with a well-intentioned but overly attentive monk pushed her to the brink of sanity. But, she must be honest, her weariness flowered in her body and mind after many years combating dark beings created, fed and fostered during the French Revolution, when rivers of blood ran from multiple massacres and public executions using Madame Guillotine.

When the winds of revolution, discontent and hunger stirred through France, she lived in the Madelonnettes Convent in the third arrondissement of Paris on the right bank of the River Seine. Her pocket named Therese belonged to the Sisters of Saint Marthe. A young and fragile novitiate, she contracted scarlet fever, and after her recovery, she described having religious visions. The girl's spirit had flown away and Ema provided animus to her body, but the story suited her purpose because the girl spent hours in contemplation alone in her cell with no one bothering her. This host provided her a place to renew her body and spirit.

Outside her avatar's body, they knew her as Madame Duplessis, brought to the convent against her will to join the Sisters of St. Lazare as were other women considered public sinners. They did not wear a habit, but concealed their faces with a black taffeta veil.

Sister Clare, the abbess' right-hand woman, and in truth the convent's unofficial Lady Abbess guarded the secret that Ema left the convent for hours. She never suspected Ema battled demons, but thought instead she acted as a spy for the Royalists, helping to smuggle out those who feared arrest and execution.

Originally, Ema came to Paris in pursuit of a dangerous demon that sought refuge on the grounds of where the Gibbet of Montfaucon once dominated the landscape. Erected in the thirteenth century, and used for three hundred years as the main gallows for the kings of France, it stood on a hill where over forty persons were hung or displayed after being executed elsewhere. The corpses rotted, sometimes for years, and carrion crows covered the structure as they pecked at the bodies. A vault lay at the bottom, and discarded bodies putrefied into bones, unless a family member paid to retrieve it for burial. The government destroyed it in 1760, but the earth it stood on could not escape the taint of suffering and blood that impregnated it.

Once there, Ema found more than just the demon she followed, and the convent became her *pied-à-terre*, until 1790 when the new government outlawed religion. Persecuted, the nuns fled or faced execution.

In 1793, the convent became the Madelonnettes prison, and Ema took her pocket and disappeared into the chaos of Paris. During those years, it took all her wits to survive as every creature craving agony congregated in the city. Two years later Therese's body succumbed to smallpox, and she spent the rest of the years, jumping from avatar to avatar. None of them survived to be sentient pockets, their soul flown into the great hereafter, and Ema combated every day to protect herself and her avatar's body.

In that moment of remembrance, Ema stopped and examined the feeling, which she strove to overlook. It came from a deep well of loneliness and fear. In an internal dialogue, she seldom paid attention to, it whispered, "Ema you are human, with desires and fears. You have overcome many obstacles, and surrendered love and companionship to protect yourself, but no matter what you do, you cannot quiet this yearning your spirit clamors for unceasingly."

Once this door opened, more disturbing thoughts burst forth. An inner voice that always spoke the truth said, "Is it fear of loneliness or boredom that pulls you from quest to quest even though you gamble with your life, and your very soul? You cannot deny the stirring deep within you when combat ensues. Whether it is your nature, or something that flowered inside you through hundreds of battles, you cannot deny it or outrun it."

Ema remembered the fall of 1798. Only a month before The Great Fear had swept through the French countryside, where peasants had wreaked havoc in revolt against their landlords. She stood looking down at the stiffening body of her last avatar as chill winds crept into a cramped garret where she lived. He was a Parisian butcher and lifelong alcoholic that succumbed after years of dissipation. Ema had taken him over out of necessity as he lay in the gutter in a drunken stupor moments from death. She coaxed a few more months of life from a human body with failing organs, not an easy feat. She decided the time had arrived for her to leave France.

As if urging her away from Paris, she received a message from Spain requesting she grant them an audience with an emissary from the Spanish Court. She later found out it concerned an aristocratic family slaughtered in their castle. Before then suspicion swirled around their involvement in occult practices. Though never denounced, the heir Don Ambrosio Figueroa y Mujica lived under a dark cloud of suspicion, believed to have orchestrated the execution of his parents and sisters as an offering to a dark lord. Clemente, his youngest brother living in a monastery escaped the bloodshed. There were no survivors, as even servants were put to the sword.

Soon after the death of his family, Don Ambrosio received a letter from the Spanish throne, ordering him to the New World. It did not take long before disturbing stories reached the ears of the Spanish King. Those who suspected his true nature sought a more permanent solution than exile.

The request made to Ema entailed traveling to New Orleans and visiting Don Ambrosio on the sugar plantation where he lived. Brother Clemente would go with her to witness the answers provided by his brother. They wanted the truth, and if the rumors were true, she should show Don Ambrosio no mercy, aristocrat or not.

Ema remembered the interview with a representative of a secret sect within the Vatican that came on behalf of the Spanish Court. She whispered to the man, "You seek to hire an executioner, but unlike one do you believe I need your permission to destroy him?" The white-haired priest gulped and stayed silent. He understood she did not seek an answer to that question, but reminded him of what the Church's place in this scheming truly was.

DIABOLIQUE
A Sibyl Novella

Plans were expedited for her trip to New Orleans aboard a Spanish courier ship. A little over a month into their voyage, the vessel dropped anchor in the harbor of San Juan, a port city in Puerto Rico, which Ema thought unusual since they stopped at the Canary Islands for supplies before crossing the Atlantic. When she asked Captain Fermin about it, he expressed his own surprise when he received last-minute instructions to stop here before leaving Tenerife. After several years of sailing an *aviso* ship, he understood not to ask too many questions. Considering the content carried in some wax-sealed letters, he thought it wise the less he knew the better for him.

Ema suspected that despite the assurance she received that her mission remained a well-kept secret; her presence on the *San Amaro* endangered every man on board.

The captain kept a handful of sailors on board, and the others went ashore with him to rendezvous with their contacts on the island. Ema refused his offer to disembark and went to her quarters as night settled over the island. She fell into a deep sleep, lulled by the movement of the vessel, and the hours slipped away.

A cut off scream overcame the regular sounds of waves slapping against the ship, and the occasional rustle of tied sails. Something heavy falling into the sea followed it. A few minutes later, the captain knocked on the door of Ema's quarters. He instructed her to keep her door locked until he returned.

She leaned against the closed door and sighed. It meant the instructions to stop in San Juan allowed something to board the ship as she suspected.

The next day he told her two sailors left behind as sentries had disappeared. A bloody handprint on a rail provided the only clue. When he questioned their shipmates, they denied any knowledge the pair planned to desert the ship. Captain Fermin suspected they did not leave of their own accord, but he could not delay any longer. They weighed anchor on the next tide and set sail for Santiago de Cuba.

Later Ema, Clemente and Captain Fermin stood on the deck discussing the mystery of the missing men.

Ema asked, "Did you ever find out why they instructed you to make this stop in San Juan?"

The captain with a quizzical expression on his face, answered, "No, and it surprised them to see me. They just dispatched letters and other messages on the regular courier ship only a week ago."

"A miscommunication, no doubt." Clemente offered.

"Perhaps." The captain answered distractedly. He suspected danger trailed after these passengers, especially the attractive widow.

In that moment, the ship's quartermaster approached them. Agitated, the man stuttered, "Captain, I… I must speak with you."

Captain Fermin excused himself, and stepped away pulling the quartermaster with him, but the man in his excitement spoke in a loud voice. The conversation carried over to where Ema and Brother Clemente stood.

"Esteban told me there is something lurking in the ship's hold. He went to gather supplies for the day's meals, and he glimpsed it lurking in the depths of the lower deck. He called it a 'devil'."

The man crossed himself and cast a grateful look at Brother Clemente.

"A devil?" The captain kept his tone calm. The cook Esteban, sailed with him for several years, and the old man made up for his lack of imagination with an ability to produce superb meals fit for a king. There was little the man feared, unless he suspected the devil's hand in it.

The quartermaster continued, "He refused to take what he needed and asked me to go in his stead."

"What did you find?"

"I went there, and I heard something."

"What did you hear? Out with it man!" The captain roared at him.

"I left because something unholy lurks in the darkness."

The captain pushed him away and stomped off towards the galley, the quartermaster trailing behind him.

Brother Clemente turned to Ema, "These sailors are quite superstitious."

"Superstitious or not, that man is scared."

A few minutes later, the captain returned and asked the monk to accompany him. "My men are disturbed because their shipmates disappeared, and they have become fearful of shadows. I believe that if you performed a blessing, it would lay to rest these fanciful notions that have them jumping at vermin scampering in the dark"

"Yes, of course, of course." Clemente agreed and followed the captain.

Ema meandered along behind the men, and when they reached the narrow stairs that descended into the hold, the captain asked her to wait for them. Ema nodded, knowing already what waited below. The cook unwittingly named the source of what stalked the lower deck of the ship. She sensed its presence vibrating in the air, like a heat wave seen in the distance.

A few minutes later, the men returned. Clemente's lips contrasted against a white ring around them when he ascended the stairs. The captain's face, taut with barely disguised fear, betrayed the fact he encountered something that shook him. Under his arm, he carried the supplies the cook asked for. He handed them off to the quartermaster who waited with Ema. The man took the supplies and left without a backwards glance.

When they reached the deck, Ema continued with the charade and asked them both what they found.

Brother Clemente with a nervous laugh assured her, "Nothing, nothing at all. I believe perhaps the food has spoiled and a disagreeable odor pervades the hold. I am sure the captain will agree with me that his crew is affected by the men that disappeared."

"Quite so, nothing for you to worry about, this dilemma has been resolved." The captain bowed and excused himself claiming other duties demanded his attention.

DIABOLIQUE
A Sibyl Novella

Ema's eyes followed his retreating figure. The captain now realized what she knew already. They were trapped on a ship with a creature intent on killing them all.

The trip between Puerto Rico and Cuba lasted six days, and the thing lurking among the supplies cast a pall of profound dread over the ship. None of the crew or the cook dared go below deck to retrieve any supplies. The two sailors ordered by the captain only descended with Brother Clemente in tow. Ema could tell he grudgingly accompanied them, because how could he dismiss their fears without proving the depth of his own misgivings.

She spent many hours sleeping in her quarters. Her body felt depleted, as if she recovered from a long illness. She had existed without a sentient avatar for over eight years, and trapped on this ship, her vulnerability became heightened to a dangerous level.

As if eager to discharge her presence, the ship plowed through the waves as brisk breezes filled the sails to the fullest. Ema stood on the deck listening to the ropes and canvas strain against the pull of the wind. She searched the horizon always hoping it remained empty.

Spain and Britain were at war and Captain Fermin constantly pulled out his spyglass to scan in every direction, to make sure that a ship did not come upon them before they could change course and speed away. He also looked out for pirates. They scoured the waters of the Antilles known as the Spanish Main. Ships carrying silver, gems, gold and hardwood sailed this watery crossroads back to Spain.

A few days later, the *San Amaro* left the Caribbean Sea and dropped anchor in a bay next to the city of Santiago. Captain Fermin explained he had no choice but to meet with city officials. His responsibility lay in making sure his delivery reached the proper hands. During war, spies were everywhere, even in a Spanish stronghold like Cuba. He had already decided to cut his stay short and take them to New Orleans for he feared death trailed behind these passengers.

The captain stood ready to climb into the waiting rowboat. He traded in his regular seafaring garb for a uniform appropriate to his mission. He wore a blue coat and waistcoat with gold buttons. Under his arm, he held a black bicorne hat that sported a cockade with Spain's national colors.

His unsmiling face left no doubt he did not want to leave Ema behind on the ship. He stared at her figure on the deck as they rowed ashore. Some men stayed behind, but most of the officers went to shore with him.

During the past six days, Ema observed that no other crew went missing, and she suspected the creature slinking in the hold waited for a chance to attack her. Several hours later, she watched the sun set in an orange ball over the horizon. The slap of waves against wood, and the murmur of conversation floated from other ships in the harbor. During the day, the pier crawled with people milling about, now it stood silent. Seagulls emptied from the sky and went off to roost somewhere. Candlelight flowered in the taverns and inns lining the wharf.

Ema ate supper with the ship's lieutenant and Brother Clemente. Afterwards, she pleaded a headache and retired to her quarters. Silence stole over the ship as the hours slipped by, and Ema heard the midshipman of the watch ring eight bells announcing midnight. She left the door unlocked, and before long, she heard a scuttling sound coming from the stairs.

She stood in a corner behind the door to her quarters and stole a glance at the lumpy figure made from bedclothes lying on the berth. Wearing only a thin muslin nightgown, she waited with her Toledo sword, Zeruko Neskamea.

Her eyes returned to the entryway which inched open, and a hand came around the edge, not human, but not animal altogether. Then a short snout, with long whiskers thrust itself in, and audibly sniffed the air. The rest of the creature crept in, and Ema confirmed her suspicion a Scrutator Demon stalked her now.

It was known for its patience and savagery. Locks and bolts could not stop them. Their stealth allowed them to glide in through doors and windows. If not slinking in the inky darkness of cellars, it perched on rooftops. They were known as biters with a predilection for newborn infants, and it was invoked with this reward.

Ema knew in her weakened state she could not open a doorway into another dimension, and so she chose her weapons wisely. The glamour she used consisted of her scent filling the entire room so it could not track her to where she stood.

This one shuffled in on elongated hind legs ending in claws. Large ears dominated a rat-like face, with a humanoid cast that nature did not allow to be conceived inside either a woman or an animal. Patches of fur were interspersed with open sores oozing dots of yellowish pus. Behind it trailed a long, hairless tail. Sharp rodent teeth protruded out the front of its mouth. It dropped to all four and crawled towards the bed, trailing an odor of decay behind it.

It screeched and chittered like a rat and pounced on the bed, clawing and shredding the blankets. Ema strode forward and arced the sword over her head, slicing down in a whirl that left a blue trail behind it. The thing lunged off the berth, and a half of its tail lay sliced and writhing among the bedclothes like a headless snake.

The demon slunk low to the ground, hissing and gibbering from the opposite corner of the compartment. It eyes shone red in the oblique darkness, and Ema knew that if she were at full strength, she could have killed the thing, instead of wounding it.

The Scrutator crouched, then stood on its hind legs, took the end of its tail dripping greenish ooze and started to suck on it. The smell of burning flesh filled the air and when it released the appendage, Ema realized it cauterized the flesh.

Ema held the pommel of the sword with both hands, and it started to glow with a turquoise light and then vibrate creating a low hum. Everything inside the room started to rattle, the demon screeched high and thin, and then blood spurted from the tip of its nostrils. It launched itself at Ema, the claws on its hands growing several inches.

DIABOLIQUE
A Sibyl Novella

Ema swung hard following its track through space, and then it rolled on the wooden planks of the floor and swiped at her ankles. She jumped away, and it crashed through the closed door.

Captain Fermin sat in a rowboat approaching the ship and stood up when he saw a bluish light flash every few seconds from the vessel. He decided to return early from a dinner party he shared with friends. Worries about Ema and his crew gave him no peace to enjoy the meal.

"Fire!" he thought and urged the two sailors rowing to put their shoulders into it.

The lantern on the rowboat swung wildly, and he flung himself to the rope ladder and sped up it. He searched for his crew. Why weren't they trying to put out the flames?

He saw another burst of blue light flash from the passage leading to Ema's quarters. He strode towards the opening, and then a creature flew out and landed with a thud on the deck. It stood on its two hind legs, and the face it turned to him reflected a human cast, but it reminded him of a rat. He heard a shout of alarm and saw the head of one sailor that rowed him over, duck back down out of sight. The captain heard him arguing with the other one telling him to get back in the rowboat.

Horror immobilized Captain Fermin; fear and disbelief anchored his feet to the spot. Throughout his seafaring years, he saw many unbelievable and disturbing scenes, but nothing like what stood on the deck of his ship.

He thought his eyes couldn't widen anymore, and then he saw a woman with long, red hair dressed only in a white nightgown run out of the passage. She held a sword in her hand that glinted in the light from the lanterns, once outside she called out "Zeruko Neskamea!" in a voice that sounded human but not quite. It held a glass-like quality to it, and he saw the creature wail in pain. The head tossed from side to side. It turned bloodied eyes to stare at the captain and he stumbled backwards.

It crouched, and he could see it preparing to spring at him. The creature leaped into the air, and something streaked inches from his head pinning the devil by the hand to the main mast of the ship. It hissed as its hand smoked and the skin started to blister.

Ema's voice sounded in his ear, "Captain, step away."

"Madame, what are you doing?" he shouted as she strode towards the creature that writhed and spit at her. An intricately carved dagger glowed with a golden light, holding the demon imprisoned. It started to gnaw at its arm, and with a few deep bites, cut through bone and flesh. It left the appendage dangling as it scampered up the mast towards the crow's nest at the top.

The breeze picked up the thin, muslin gown around Ema's body and it flowed in the wind, as did her hair. Dumbfounded by the shock of what he just experienced, the captain gazed for the first time on the face he usually saw through a widow's veil. More lovely than he imagined, he wanted to protect her, especially now in a moment of danger. He shrugged his coat off and attempted to place it around her shoulders.

"Wait." She said in a low voice, putting a hand on his arm.

She stepped to where the fingers wriggled as if still attached to the body. She pulled the dagger loose, and with a swift movement of her wrist, she threw the arm over the side into the seawater. From the top of the mast, the demon screeched and chittered.

Ema proceeded to the railing, the captain at her side, and they saw the thing boil and sizzle on top of the water. It became nothing, and then a flaming carcass dropped from the mast overhead and splashed into the ocean. It flailed about, a dreadful smell drifting on the wind. Flesh disappeared, and only a skull and blackened bones bobbed in the water and then sunk below the surface.

Then Ema accepted his coat, and she whispered to him, "We must talk.

2. Hunting the Hunter

Ema sat in the captain's quarters and heard him shouting orders. He returned and told her how he found the crew, including Brother Clemente hiding in the galley. The lieutenant convinced the men not to abandon the ship and row to shore. One of them saw the creature as it made its way to Ema's quarters and raised the alarm with the rest of the crew. They forcibly dragged the monk with them using him as a human talisman.

He poured a cup of Madeira wine for each of them and sat across from Ema.

"Dios mio," the captain murmured, "I don't know whether to burn this ship, scuttle it or keep sailing it."

"Captain Fermin," Ema responded to him, placing a reassuring hand on his arm, "there is nothing wrong with this ship. I cannot give you the explanation you deserve, but I assure you that creature is here following me."

"You?"

"Yes, I suspect you know that I am not a poor widow sailing to New Orleans for a fresh start in life."

A half-crooked smile eased the tension out of his face. "No, especially when the instructions for delivering you to New Orleans came from the Spanish court itself. I have learned after many years, not to ask questions."

"Ah, a wise man indeed."

"Does the monk know the truth? He argued with me, insisting he wanted to see you in person."

"No he does not, he believes he does but his knowledge is limited."

"I thought as much."

"My advice is to tell the crew as little as possible and let Brother Clemente bless the ship once we are underway. When you return to Madrid, tell them you saw nothing, only something that cast itself into the sea from the crow's nest."

"Very well," he responded, and cleared his throat with uncertainty before continuing, "I would not ask questions of this nature from a lady, but I believe you are the only one who can give me the answers I seek."

Ema nodded to him to proceed.

"What is that creature?"

"It is a demon, and like many creatures that originate in hell they are susceptible to iron and salt. A connection exists between its arm and the rest of its body, which is why when I cast it into the ocean, the rest of the body immolated."

"This demon is here because of you. How can this be?"

Ema's green eyes studied the lined face of the middle-aged, bearded man who sat before her. "Captain, I could give you a lengthy and complicated answer, which would burden you both spiritually and in the material world. I believe that you understand sometimes ignorance is the safest choice, and in this case, it is."

The man stood up and paced back and forth with his hands behind his back. He stopped and stared at Ema, "Yes, I agree, and for that reason I will not ask how a lady like you can handle a sword better than most men I know, and throw a dagger quite a distance to pin a moving target to the mast."

Ema stayed silent. Captain Fermin knew the conversation had ended.

"Very well," he murmured.

"Captain, I have one last favor to ask of you."

"I am yours to command."

"Keep the crew on board, and we should weigh anchor and leave for New Orleans with the first outgoing tide."

"I know you have good reason to ask this. We will leave within the day."

"Thank you Captain, and if you could send someone to my quarters with fresh bedclothes, I will return your coat with them."

The *San Amaro* sailed away in the early morning hours of the following day. If the winds continued to favor them, the remaining leg of the journey was almost over.

The captain met with his officers and gave them instructions on how to handle the crew that were a fearful lot. They were not cowards, and were prepared to engage in hand-to-hand combat, but not with the supernatural.

Ema kept dressing as a widow, she found mourning for a dead, if mythical, husband kept men at bay, and avoided conversations from strangers. Brother Clemente hovered over her, and questioned her about what happened that night, but she told him she stayed in her quarters behind a locked door. This satisfied him, but she could tell doubt still swirled in his mind.

If Ema could have willed the ship to plow through the water faster she would have, because she could not escape a niggling suspicion that accompanied her throughout the days. On the morning of the third day, her doubts were confirmed. She stood at her usual spot on the main deck. She saw when one officer approached the captain who stood on the forecastle scanning the horizon with his spyglass. The captain hurried off with the officer below deck.

She did not have long to wait before the captain approached her. From across the deck Brother Clemente looked at them with eyes full of suspicion.

"The remains of a sailor have been found in the lower deck. Among his bloody entrails we found his rosary, otherwise they could not have identified him."

"I am sorry you have lost a member of your crew." Ema answered with a thoughtful expression on her face.

"You are not surprised."

"Captain Fermin, the demon we destroyed, attacked me in my quarters first. I chopped off its tail, and I now realize that this piece of it didn't burn up, but regenerated into another creature."

"Another one?" he exclaimed in alarm.

"Do not let your crew descend into the lower deck unless they have to, and not by themselves."

"What if Brother Clemente goes to face this evil?"

Ema glanced at the monk, and then stared into Captain Fermin's eyes, "He does not have enough faith to combat this creature; better ignorant than dead. Lay a trail of salt across the entryway and pray the weather remains fair."

The man studied her, nodded and strode away. Ema's eyes followed him, and she wished she could tell him that only her weakness prevented her from killing the Scrutator demon, but for once, she admitted to her limitations.

Now, only hours from reaching New Orleans, the captain told her another sailor died, and she knew the creature hoped to lure her into the bowels of the ship. However, sacrificing herself could not bring back the dead, and more than likely condemn the entire ship.

The *San Amaro* dropped anchor an hour before sunset. Several hours later, Ema descended to a waiting rowboat. The captain could convince only one sailor to row her ashore. A large crucifix hung around his neck, and only the promise of a hefty reward for the job convinced him to take the woman to shore.

Captain Fermin bowed to her and said, "God go with you, madam. I do this with deep misgivings, but you have convinced me this is the best course of action."

"What I tell you now captain is only for your ears, and do not repeat it to anyone, even your wife or family. If the Inquisition calls you before them, say, 'I am under the protection of *La Dama Roja*'".

"The Red Lady?"

"Yes, this information will end the audience at once."

A speculative glint entered the man's eyes. "Whom exactly did he have on board?" he asked himself.

Ema stepped down the rope ladder into the rocking rowboat. The sailor swung the paddles and strained to push the boat through the water. A small lantern swayed with the motion of the boat. Far off danced the lights showing where the city of New Orleans waited. Shadows played across their faces, and only the sound of splashing oars could be heard.

When the sailor across from her heard what Ema discerned moments before, he let go of the oars and threw himself headfirst to the bottom of the boat, praying aloud as he crossed his hands over his head.

The sound of flapping wings drew closer and Ema gazed up and saw what at first glance resembled a large bird, except that a human face hung in the air glaring down at her. In its talons, it carried a Scrutator Demon. In that moment, Ema knew she had no chance of surviving an attack from two antagonists. She stood up, grabbed the lantern and threw it at what she recognized as a harpy.

Her aim proved true, and the projectile hit the creature full in the face. It did what Ema hoped for in that moment; it dropped the demon into the sea, whereupon it screamed in agony as the sea swallowed it.

Ema shouted at the sailor to pray in silence. Within seconds, nothing else came from the prostrate man. She strained her hearing because the harpy, known as a vengeful being, could not be far off from where they floated on the water. She reminded herself that she was reduced to throwing objects at an attacker. All because she emptied herself of the energy, necessary to pull her weapons into this dimension. Ema feared that if she tried to bring them to her side, she would faint.

Out of the darkness, the harpy dove at her and she barely ducked her head in time. A nightmare thing, cobbled together with an emaciated woman's head surrounded by flowing hair, a human torso and upper legs. Instead of arms, feathered wings sprouted from her shoulders. Vultures' claws replaced her human feet.

Ema knew its intention was not to knock her into the sea. It meant to blind her and then scoop her off somewhere to endure torture and then feed on her. These creatures suffered from an insatiable hunger.

She pulled out her dagger, Iron Horse, from a belt on her waist and waited to inflict a wound that could drive the harpy away for a time, allowing her to reach the shore. Then she heard an ululation never uttered by a human throat. She crouched ready to strike out. Off in the east, the sky started to lighten, and she saw the whirr and movement of the harpy's wings as it stretched out its talons aimed at her face.

Just as she sprung up, a sudden movement rocked the rowboat and Ema pitched forward into the water. The coolness of it enveloped her, and the cloth of the gown clung to her legs and she sunk lower into the inky darkness. She stuck the dagger back in her belt, and tried with failing strength to swim to the surface, but she lost her sense of direction. Ema thought at least the harpy couldn't reach her under the water, and then she felt strong hands grab her waist before she lost consciousness.

3. Beggars Can't Be Choosers

Ema breathed in, and she heard the slap of water against rocks. Her body swayed back and forth, as waves swirled around her. The fecund smell of the swampland filled her nostrils. She opened her eyes and two silver dollars inside a blue face stared down at her.

The mermaid spoke to her in a sibilant whisper, "Sibylline, why are you chasing death?"

"Sister, it appears that way doesn't it?" Ema answered her.

"Considering that you were trying to battle a harpy, leads me to believe you are just being foolish instead of seeking your own destruction."

The mermaid placed a webbed hand across Ema's cheek. Slick with water, she could feel the warmth of life throbbing through her. "You are weak and sick; an easy target for the enemies that always trail after you."

"I have no one to blame but myself. I foolishly traversed the ocean when I should have bided my time."

"You will need one to rest yourself within their body. Men gather many times near this place to battle one another over a slight to their honor. These men are others who chase death, as if in ignorance of its finality."

"You mean they come here for duels?"

"Yes, and I hear the sounds of approaching horses. So close to dawn it can only mean one thing."

"Thank you Melusine whenever you need my help you need only to seek me out and I shall come to your side."

The mermaid answered her, "No, I am still in your debt."

Ema had saved her several hundred years before when she became entangled in a fisherman's net in the Mediterranean Sea. Normally Melusine could have freed herself, but a child grew inside of her, the one child she could produce in her lifetime. In the throes of bringing it forth, in the custom of the Mer people, she went off by herself. She struggled on the deck of a ship, while the fisherman debated how to kill her. Her power to subdue and mesmerize, evaporated at this solitary moment. Ema, hidden in one of the fishermen freed her, but only after a terrific fight with most of the crew.

"What happened to the sailor in the rowboat?"

"One of us pushed him back to his ship. No doubt he will have a wonderful tale to tell his companions."

The sound of men's voices drifted over to where they were. "Go now." Ema urged the mermaid. Melusine nodded, and the iridescent scales below her hips caught the morning sun and with a flip of her fanlike tail, she disappeared below the surface.

Ema pulled herself up the embankment and peeked through tall reeds towards a group of men that came towards where she hid. She slid back into the water. Shivering, she slipped off her sodden clothes. With a small pulse of energy, she pushed the dagger into another dimension.

She heard the rules of the duel explained. After taking a shot at each other, if neither bullet found their mark, reconciliation became a way where both men could claim satisfaction on their quarrel. She peered over again and saw a tall, younger man, a proud Creole no doubt. His opponent, a short, plump man at least twenty-five years his senior paced back and forth. Balding, his fair hair lay damp with sweat upon his forehead. Ema saw a dark cloud hovering around him, and she knew that Death waited to take him on this day. The seconds and a surgeon stood off to one side.

Ema ducked back and summoned the most energy she could raise because she knew she only had seconds to jump into this man once his soul departed. The countdown began and then the rapport of both pistols followed.

The sound of running feet and then exclamations of dismay followed, "Henry, my God Henry! Doctor, he's been hit. I think he's dead. Examine him."

Another voice replied, "His pulse is ebbing, the bullet is in the right side, I fear it has hit some important blood vessels".

Ema peered once more and saw the surgeon drape a coat over the older man's face. He straightened up and spoke intently to a distraught man that appeared to be his second. The Creole's face, proud and disdainful showed no concern. He put on his coat, flicking off imaginary dirt from the sleeves.

Time came to a standstill as Ema changed her vibration, entered and meshed inside the man's body. At once, she saw the bullet did not kill him but a damaged heart did. This physical impairment she could fix for at least two years. The man's soul left and his body kept breathing and functioning at its barest minimum to stay alive. The only animus and personality came from Ema.

The Creole named Noel Girod called across the field, "My sister's honor has been restored. She would never consider a suitor like him. Rather she should remain unmarried than join with a man of doubtful origins."

Ema determined the time arrived to startle these fine gentlemen.

The draped body moaned, and the conversation ceased. Another sound came from the man, and the doctor ripped the coat away and examined a body, which he could have sworn lay dead only a few moments ago. His second crouched over him and then shouted to have the carriage brought to where they were.

In short order, they transported the wounded man to his home, which lay closer to the scene of the duel. The surgeon, Dr. Destrehan removed a bullet from his shoulder. He stayed by his patient's side the rest of the day and instructed his housekeeper, Mrs. Manson how to care for him. Unmarried, his patient's care fell to this woman and several servants living in the household. His second, Nicholas Semple, a business partner only left the house that evening when the doctor assured him the wounded man's survival was assured.

Dr. Destrehan checked on his patient during the following days and grew satisfied with the progress he made. Nevertheless, he could not deny the man's subdued demeanor puzzled him. Perhaps a brush with death made him realize how easily a man could lose his life over a misunderstanding.

Ema became acquainted with her avatar's life and habits. His name was Henry Beasley, a successful merchant from New York, who foresaw the opportunities that awaited in New Orleans as a port city with access to the Mississippi River. He collaborated with Nicholas Semple a native of the city that opened many doors for him.

She went through his papers including his personal diary and gathered enough information to garner an accurate picture of him. He was a competent businessman but greedy. No romantic, his recent decision to marry a young bride, became a business venture to be negotiated for the best outcome. The woman should be fair of face, wealthy and able to produce an heir in a short amount of time. Ema found a list of potential ladies. Among them, the name of Natalie Girod had an entry next to it, "I suspect Holbet is in love with her."

Ten days later, this man presented himself at Beasley's house on the corner of Gravier and Magazin streets. William Holbet captained the American schooner *Syren*. Tall, middle-aged with gray streaking his beard and hairline he stood erect and unsmiling before Henry. He turned over an itemization of goods for sale waiting on the ship. The list included, ginghams, velvets, tin plates, tobacco, country sugar, pickled salmon in kegs, New York crackers and Havana cigars.

Captain Holbet appeared uncomfortable speaking to Beasley. He reviewed the items and said to Holbet, "Very well, stop by the office and have Semple set a sale date for next week at the Exchange Coffee House."

Holbet pulled his bicorne hat out from under his arm and set it on his head. He nodded curtly, turned and left. He never asked Henry about his brush with death, confirming he knew that Natalie had been the reason for the duel.

Ema reminded herself that she could not alter her avatar's behavior too much. Henry Beasley, before the duel wouldn't have given a farthing for the man's distress, on the contrary, he had made plans to marry the woman Holbet loved.

As Henry Beasley's body healed so did Ema, but caution tempered her actions. She knew after spending several years with pockets not in the best of health, her recovery would be slow. Added to this, she found herself in a city she did not know, without any allies and no idea whom her enemies were.

Ema sent for her belongings being held at the Ursuline convent. She sent a purposely vague message to Brother Clemente, letting him know she felt unwell and recuperated at the home of an acquaintance.

One evening she sat in Henry's bedroom, reading the local newspaper by candlelight. Henry's body lay motionless in a bed draped with mosquito netting. A short article made mention on the disappearance of Don Ambrosio Figueroa y Mujica. The circumstances of his absence were unknown, and the story hinted at a looming scandal. In the meantime, a steward continued to run Belle Mer the sugarcane plantation he owned.

Her mind traveled to that time she lived on the treacherous streets of Paris during The Terror. Those hard years crippled her now from confronting Don Ambrosio before he fled New Orleans. The toll it took demanded time to heal. She had witnessed the unleashed hostilities that befell the populace. Not only aristocrats became victims, but many other innocent victims ended up with their head stuck on a pole and paraded through the streets. Anyone suspected of counterrevolutionary thoughts could find themselves in front of a firing squad, being beaten or weighted and thrown into the water to drown, without benefit of a trial. Even those were a farce. Mob mentality ruled, and neighbor turned against neighbor, quick to point a finger because they wanted to avenge a personal slight. Those had been savage years.

However, the chaos helped to mask much of her activity. Those who fed their thirst for blood by orchestrating the death of humans while under the direction of demonic possession met untimely deaths or just disappeared. Some thought that the mention of *La Dame Rouge* referred to the guillotine, but those who were familiar with occult and esoteric subjects knew better, and wisely did not pursue inquiry into what happened to these *"citoyens"* lest they come to her attention.

Two weeks later, Henry Beasley gave his entire household staff the day off. Once the house had emptied, Ema left Henry's body in what resembled a deep sleep in his bed. She donned her widow's weeds and visited the solicitors that represented the Figueroa estate. Using her former identity when she lived in Paris as Madame Duplessis, she presented the letters from the Spanish court turning the Figueroa properties over to her authority. They must have caught wind of this change beforehand because they appeared unsurprised. They gave assurances of their total cooperation in all matters. Their recommendation was to keep the steward who had held the post for over ten years.

The next day Henry reappeared at his office. Nicholas Semple reviewed all the business transactions that took place while he recuperated.

Then offhandedly he dug for the story behind Captain Holbet and Natalie Girod. Nicholas told him the story of a young woman unlucky in love. It turned out Natalie, long past the acceptable marriage age according to Creole standards, was doomed to become the family spinster. During her early youth, no suitor met the high standards of her aristocratic family, and the years slipped by with no ring on her finger. A few months ago, a chance meeting at a New Orleans park stirred a romance between Holbet and Natalie that her family quashed once they caught wind of it.

Nicholas remarked to Henry, "I know you overlooked her age as a potential bride because of her connections and wealth, but you should have known her family would never find favor with you as a bridegroom. I believe her brother challenged you because he wants any potential suitors to understand what will happen if anyone else comes to call on Mademoiselle Natalie."

"Do you think it scared Holbet off from pursuing her?"

"No I don't, and I will tell you sincerely Henry, I believe she is in love with him. However, he knows that he doesn't have much to offer her. He suffered enough heartbreak when he lost his wife and two children to typhus five years ago. When you bought the *Syren* to save him from his debts, and allowed him to stay as her captain, one could say is the only stroke of good luck that's visited him in years."

Not forgetting the role he played as the greedy businessman, Henry commented, "Quite a sad story. Let us speak now of the ships expected this week."

4. Something Evil

During those days that Ema used Henry Beasley's body as a pocket, and she reconstituted her energy, she never forgot that someone either at the Spanish court or at the Vatican betrayed her.

Prior to leaving Europe, she did her own investigation. She found out the nature of the beast that awaited her in New Orleans. Don Ambrosio Figueroa y Mujica could only be one thing, a vampire, a powerful one. For years, he had involved himself in murder and necromancy, dragging his family into many dark practices, but the price of his final initiation by a sadistic lord demanded the murder of his parents and two younger sisters.

Ema knew that another vampire had preceded Don Ambrosio in the Louisiana Territory. For fifty years, rumors reached her that a vampire came to the New World, when French Louisiana grew along the banks of the Mississippi River. However, during those years, the colonial population comprised many undesirable characters. Trappers, gold hunters and deported galley slaves were sent over as soldiers. If these or the natives were hunted by a vampire, no outcry reached the French court. Nevertheless, under Spanish rule the population swelled as immigrants came from Spain, the Canary Islands and the Spanish colonies. Commerce on the Mississippi flourished, as did New Orleans. Strange deaths and tales of entire families being wiped out could not be ignored, but then the stories died out. Only whispered anecdotes of a creature haunting the swamps circulated through New Orleans society.

December 1794 a fire swept through the city destroying over two hundred buildings. It was in the winter months that followed that new stories of atrocities reached the Spanish court and the Vatican. They coincided with Don Ambrosio's arrival in New Orleans. Secret meeting were held to discuss the growing suspicion that they had not exported a debauched, murderous, aristocrat, but a dark being who could no longer claim to be human.

Ema ran across French inquisitiveness in these rumors, which led her to believe that Louisiana might soon return to French rule. Perhaps her saboteur originated in France.

Henry Beasley known to be tight-fisted with his money surprised his housekeeper Mrs. Manson when he again gave the entire staff the day off. She was baffled by the change in his habits. He ate different foods, in smaller portions. He hardly touched liquor and sought out his bed shortly after dinner.

Ema again left Henry's body supine in bed. She had decided to stay in New Orleans for a time, and this necessitated establishing her own home. There was an added urgency to her actions as she recognized that Henry's body could not be used as long as she originally estimated.

A week before, Henry bought a small Creole cottage on Bourgoine Street. He placed it under the name of Madame Duplessis. The agents who handled the transaction smiled assuming Mr. Beasley bought it for his mistress, especially after he ordered furnishings and carpets delivered to the address. Another gift was a gray, Andalusian mare just arrived from Spain, along with a finely stitched sidesaddle. The rumor mill told them everything about the duel with Girod. But who better than a favorite lover to help one recover?

Ema used that day to tour the small house. It had stood empty for several years since it was believed to be haunted. Built of brick and elevated to withstand flooding, steps led to two sets of French doors, graced by tall, narrow dormer windows that were shuttered. A half story upstairs she decided to make her bedroom. Behind the cottage, a separate building housed the kitchen and the cook's quarters. The property also included a small stable with a field that could be used to graze the horse.

As Ema strolled through the garden, she sensed a frisson in the air, and the words, "Help me," drifted to her. So it did deserve its reputation for being haunted after all; time enough later to discover who and why.

Henry ordered servants to prepare the home for her, and once it had been readied, she moved in. She hired a neighborhood orphan named Pepin to care for the horse that she named Alegria. He slept in a narrow loft in the stable.

Early one morning he readied the mare and helped Ema mount. She tossed him a coin when he pointed out how well he had polished the saddle, and he grinned at her as she cantered out into the leafy avenue.

A pleasant ride through the Vieux Carre brought her to the spires of St. Louis Cathedral. She dismounted and came into an entrance portico where the smell of incense hung heavy in the air. A man waited for her there.

Père Antoine stood in the dimness, studying the woman's face though the widow's veil she wore. Over twenty years ago, he came to New Orleans as an official of the Spanish Inquisition, now he served as the church's pastor.

His voice was low as he said, "Word of your coming preceded you from someone who has my complete trust."

"I have come for many reasons, but there were grave concerns expressed about Don Ambrosio Figueroa y Mujica."

"Ah yes Don Ambrosio, among the genteel population he's considered a dissipated man with a sordid family history that even the marriage-hungry mamas cannot overlook. Among those that he need not impress there is only one thing he instills, it is an absolute fear."

"Why?" Ema asked.

"If he were cruel and mendacious, those are traits I am well acquainted with, and it would not disturb me as profoundly as the stories I have heard about this man. They refer to him as *Le Diable*, and in a literal sense. Rumors from the maroon settlements are that he drinks the blood of the living. They say he is a vampire. He avoids his plantation Belle Mer because of an old woman named Tante Ange. In her youth, she banished another evil being that decimated the slaves under the cover of night. Many believed they were running away, but instead they were being drained of blood and left to rot in the swamp. That was many years ago. Now she is free, and lives nearby with her family. No doubt he still fears she could do the same to him."

"The newspapers have noted his absence from the city, coincidentally after my arrival." Ema pointed out.

"There is no coincidence in this. Just because he disappeared does not mean he has left. Many wicked things lurk in this place. When the summer arrives, those who can leave, escape the city and the threat of fever. But those left behind are especially vulnerable."

"I have decided to stay in New Orleans. I need a woman to keep house for me. Could you refer someone trustworthy?"

"I will speak to a midwife who knows of many who could fill the post. Her name is Blanche Beaupre; she is a *gens de couleur libre.*"

"The house is on Bourgoine Street. Please tell her I need someone who is discreet."

"I will send word to her tomorrow. She knows who is pestilence-salted and can survive should the fever descend upon us."

The priest turned inquiring eyes to Ema, whose attention shifted to a bent figure kneeling at a small prie-dieu with several candles lit before a statue of the Virgin Mary.

"I do not mean to offend you, but there is great danger in this undertaking. Your intentions might be the best, but I am not sure those who sent you explained the nature of the evil that waits for night to fall." Père Antoine tried to gauge if this woman understood that prayers alone would not suffice.

"Père Antoine, I have more than intentions."

The man raised his eyebrows, wondering what she meant. He did not have long to wait. Ema turned and strode towards the figure kneeling with bowed head. She passed by a font full of holy water, and she cupped and filled her hand with the liquid. With a swift movement, she flung it at the figure.

The dark silhouette turned and hissed, levitating itself in the air. The priest stumbled back when in the church's gloom he saw the thing's eyes glowed red inside of a horrible skull-like face. Black teeth surrounded a rictus grin, and yellow skin stretched tight across the bones of the face. Spindly legs and arms writhed around it like a spider. The thing then cackled and thick drool slobbered to the floor beneath it.

"Damned veil!" Ema snarled as she ripped it off her head.

The thing hissed, "Begone woman, I have come for him." A bony finger pointed behind her.

Ema glanced over her shoulder, saw the priest fall to his knees, bowing his head with closed eyes, and pray in Latin. The odor of decay grew as the black, shroud-like clothing of the dead thing stirred in a non-existent breeze. It advanced on both of them and started to clack its rotten teeth.

Ema dipped her fingers in the holy water and flicked droplets at the creature's face. The parchment-like skin blistered, and the bone poked through a smoking slit. The scarlet eyeballs once riveted on Père Antoine, swiveled to the woman and it snarled with rage and hate.

"Now that I have your attention, I have two words for you." The creature advanced on her, the stink of corruption increasing and hissing on different levels emanating from around it. "*Daemonium cedo!*" Ema's voice echoed clear as a bell, and the thing halted. The voices of the unseen things that susurrated a moment before diminished as if falling into a pit. The entity floated backwards, the twin lights of its eyes flickering and dimming.

"You must want him badly if you dare to come so close to a holy place." Ema's voice still echoed as her words hung in the air like the last notes of a beautiful aria.

The entity screeched. Its shriveled, blackened tongue danced in the orifice of its mouth.

Ema pointed her finger at the doors leading into the church, and they slammed shut; others throughout the church thundered closed as well.

Two cherubs who decorated the pedestal of the font, with a grinding noise detached themselves from the stone. The pockmarked appearance of their bodies smoothed out, and their flesh filled in to polished smoothness. Their wings feathered in with different hues of blue, and as they fluttered in the air, they grew. They became tall, muscled and strong, wearing armor, each holding a shield and sword. Their skin shimmered in oscillating colors.

"Sibyllina, command us." They said in unison.

"Protect him." She indicated Père Antoine, who rose and stood against the wall clutching the crucifix he wore around his neck. He crossed himself.

One angel, pulled the priest into his embrace, and guided him inside the main building of the cathedral. The other one dissolved into the air, only blue lights dancing in the space where it once stood.

The dark being who gyrated in hellish delight only moments before tried to leave the entrance to the cathedral, but found it could not. Tethered by an invisible cord it lunged forward, only to be pulled back.

Ema advanced from the porch into the interior of the church, a blue stream of light shot out from her forefinger and lassoed the being, pulling it inside as it struggled. The thing screamed in a dozen voices and timbres, resisting entry to a place anathema to it.

"No!" It wailed now in one, deep voice.

Puzzled, Ema admitted she made a mistake. She assumed this creature followed her, but instead it came for Père Antoine. The question remained why target this priest after so many years of living in New Orleans. The answer was clear; someone wished to sabotage the meeting between her and the pastor.

"I must return," it wailed, "I must return soon."

Ema tugged on the blue neon lasso that held it in place, and it squealed louder than a pig being led to slaughter.

"Who sent you?"

"They called me, with the drums. They pulled the master from the servant." The creature complained. It contorted, unable to break free.

"And who is your servant?"

"Micajah, Micajah Harpe."

"How long have you been with him?"

"Thirty years, only an instant, but I must return soon."

Ema knew why it wanted to return to the man it possessed for so many years. Without a maleficent spirit to guide him, the man's cunning, luck some might call it, would disappear. It knew that if it were absent too long, there would be no human to return to.

"You will come with me." Ema said.

"No!" The thing wailed louder.

Ema strode inside the church and pulled it along as it howled. "If you do not answer my question, I will take you to the altar." Ema indicated where Père Antoine waited with both angels.

The red eyeballs, suspended in black orbits even without the benefit of facial features, gleamed with terror.

"There is so much light there, too much light."

"Answer the question I asked."

"They summoned me because they know my name, the name I cannot remember." The creature twisted and hissed. "Like a wind it tore me away."

A knowing expression filled Ema's face. "You are no demon wretch, but a human spirit."

"No!"

"A demon does not forget its name, never. Why were you sent here?"

"A moment of insanity. So much evil can be accomplished against others or oneself, in a moment of insanity." The grimace of the thin cracking lips returned, "I remember insanity, the constant of my existence."

"Why now?"

"Sacrifice, the time of sacrifice is near. The time of his death."

"Whose death?"

With its one free, arm it pointed at the altar, at the statue of the crucified Christ. "His." A hollow screaming laugh echoed from the dark thing.

Père Antoine stepped down, with his bodyguards on either side. "Lent is upon us. *Quadragesima.*"

"Release me, the drums are calling."

Ema stared at the creature writhing in agony, being summoned to obey one without mercy.

"Let us see who you really are." Ema brought the creature closer. The stench of death became replaced by the sweet smell of roses. It stopped twisting, the glowing eyes glued to Ema's face.

"Show yourself." Ema whispered to it.

DIABOLIQUE
A Sibyl Novella

Muscle and skin started to reconstitute itself over the frame of bones. The blackened shroud enfolding its body started to lighten, returning to the original color of the cloth. It became an old withered woman.

"Remember." Ema ordered.

"No." the woman wailed.

"Remember." Ema repeated.

The skin of the face became smoother, and a thatch of white, frizzy hair darkened to a caramel color. The sunken eyes plumped and freckles splattered across the bridge of the nose, but the look of madness could not be denied in this younger version. She became a short, squat woman with crooked teeth.

Ema waved her hand, and the woman stopped struggling, the insanity erased from her face.

"What is your name?"

"I never received a name." The woman answered in a monotone voice, with a slight Scottish burr. "My mother would have named me Abigail if she had a mind to do so, but her brain became diseased, and madness dictated her actions. Created in violence within her womb, the spirit of insanity fused within my bones. She bore me in a place where they kept those like us, too violent, easily aroused to kill and maim. A dark spirit destroyed our lives, where there was no mercy, kindness or love. I was darkness. I am darkness."

In a blur, too quick for the eye to follow, Ema caught the woman by the back of the neck and at first glance, it appeared she tore the woman asunder. To one side she threw the actual image of the woman, and in her fist, she held a lizard-like thing that hissed and spit at Ema.

Père Antoine grunted and retreated to the altar.

One angel stooped and helped the woman. She stood next to the tall figure, staring at it with wondering eyes. The angel placed a protective arm around her shoulders.

The lizard's tail swished back and forth, and for all its animal aspect, a preternatural intelligence filled its eyes as it spoke, "Mighty Sibyl, another soul you have saved from damnation. But you cannot save them all; even you cannot be in every place at once."

It seemed strange to hear a four-foot reptilian thing speak in an intelligible voice. Ema recognized this outer shell as a disguise, just one of its many. It tried to imitate one of the life forms of this plane, but it could never do so, only a corrupted version.

"Nor would I want to be. There is no escape from Divine Order, for no one, or nothing, even creatures like you."

The mottled green skin darkened, and it drew it lips back again as it hissed in a guttural voice. It tried to break the grip Ema forced on its neck.

"Today is a good day," she surmised, "I will save two from damnation."

"Send me back to hell."

"No, I shall give you the reward you deserve, not the one you desire."

31

Ema tossed the thing through the air, and the other angel caught it again by its neck. It wriggled and screamed as it sizzled within the angel's fingers. The other one, still holding Abigail's hand wend its way back to Ema. It took her hand and kissed the top of it. "My Lady, we are never far from your voice, we will come to your aid if you ever summon us."

Ema bowed her head and then smiled at the angel, its violet shimmering eyes shifting with ever changing shades of lavender and mauve. "Guard the priest, they will come again for him and perhaps this time disguised in another form."

Under the baptismal font, a light shimmered and then an opening materialized with stairs leading downward into a golden place where details became hazy. Each angel walked towards it, one leading the woman, the other, the demonic being that still struggled. The group descended into the depths. Their images became transparent and merged with the stone, and then there was nothing. Only a flood of sweet incense smell filled the church. Candles burning low sparked back to life with a leaping flame.

The priest trailed after Ema as she went back to where her black veil lay on the floor. She draped it over her face.

The priest's voice sounded contrite, "Forgive my impudence, my ignorance."

"There is nothing to forgive, Mon Père."

He glanced at the font full of holy water; the cherubs once more adorned the pedestal.

He murmured, "If I did not know my eyes could not lie to me, I would not believe what I have seen this day."

The doors swung open, and she stepped back out to the entrance portico. The afternoon sun cast pockets of shade throughout the gardens surrounding the cathedral. Pedestrians strolled along unaware of what took place inside the church. Far off the sparkle from the river glimmered in the sunlight

"Père Antoine, I urge you to keep our secret. You know where to find me. Do not forget to speak to Madame Beaupre on my behalf."

"No Madame, I shall not."

Ema meandered towards a teenage boy who waited with Alegria under the branches of a shady tree. She knew now her presence in the city was no longer a secret. Like a fisherman who knows a slack line means he's lost the fish, whoever sent this creature knew their emissary did not exist any longer. Opening a doorway between dimensions as she did, set up a thrumming in the metaphysical world, which they recognized as something beyond the power of the priest.

Père Antoine watched as she mounted the horse. Even a man bound with a vow of celibacy recognized her allure, with her titian hair and green eyes. How did this woman become a warrior adept at combating Evil? What heavenly authority allowed her to summon Angels? He hoped introspection and prayer might give him an answer.

The boy handed her the reins and a black tricorn hat, which she placed on her head. She gave him a coin, and then cantered the horse away to join the carriages, riders and pedestrians on the Vieux Carre. Soon her figure melted into the tide of humanity, and the old priest lost her from view.

He stepped back into the murkiness of the portico. Only now did he realize how evil could hide itself in a multitude of guises. The Sibyl as they called her in the letter he received had won a new ally on this day. With a bowed head, and deep in thought he made his way to his quarters.

Brother Clemente Figueroa stood in the shadow cast by the huge cathedral that towered above him, watching the object of his obsession. Madame Duplessis the captain called her, but he knew she had another name, a secret name.

He thought of her always. Part of him wanted to believe she came here for him, but he knew her whispered exchange with Père Antoine did not include a mention of his name. Intrigue swirled around her, like the black, gauzy veil she wore. In his dreams, he saw the flash of her green eyes, and the discontent of his vows chafed at him like sackcloth.

His parents forced him to take religious vows when he harbored no vocation in his heart, but his family's ambition knew no bounds. They wanted one of their own to ascend through the Church. Being a younger son, with no promise of inheriting any lands never worried him. Drawing and painting fueled the entirety of his ambitions.

The vague discontent he lived with blossomed into a desire that consumed him. Not even the fear of hell could alter his plans. He swore he would be part of her life in one way or another.

5. The Absent Puppet Master

Micajah Harpe measured six feet, four inches. His family emigrated from Scotland to the Carolinas, when Britain still ruled America as a colony. At the onset of the Revolutionary War, he along with his cousin Wiley Harpe joined a rape gang, which preyed on patriot colonists. They cut a wide swath of murder and destruction in their path and even joined the Chickamauga and Cherokee to attack the patriot settlements. They lived with them for a dozen years in a village named Nickajack. They were known for disemboweling their victims so they could fill the body cavity with stones and sink the corpses in rivers or creeks.

Both men killed their own children, including Micajah who took an infant daughter and slammed her against a tree trunk because of her incessant crying.

Starting in 1797 they went on a spree, plundering and murdering any who stood in their path. They outsmarted posses and lawmen sent after them. Both of them bragged of killing over forty men, women and children, but everyone knew the number fell short of the truth. They gambled that the devil's luck, which kept them alive for so many years, would continue to do so.

In the spring of 1799, something changed.

It started when the governor of Kentucky offered a $300 reward for their capture, dead or alive.

That summer Mrs. Stegall stayed at home with her infant son and a male houseguest. Her husband had left on business. The Harpes visited the house and killed the houseguest, slit the throat of Mrs. Stegall's four-month-old son, and when she tried to intervene, they killed her.

In August 1799, a posse pursued them; Moses Stegall numbered among them. He claimed he wanted vengeance for the murder of his family, but others whispered that he once befriended the Harpes and held a portion of their money. He wanted to keep the booty for himself, but feared their betrayal. He even sacrificed his own wife and son to get the law on his side.

The posse caught up with the men, and Micajah "Big" Harpe fell when a bullet wounded him. His cousin did not stay to help and instead fled into the countryside. Moses Stegall unsheathed a long sharp knife, took a fully conscious Micajah Harpe by the hair and slowly sawed off his head. He then impaled it on a tree branch where it rotted down to a skull. The place became known as Harpe's Head.

For years afterwards, the place of his beheading earned a reputation for being haunted. The ghost fit his description: a tall man with matted red hair, a face distorted and twisted with indescribable horror and agony, a vacant stare, devoid of intelligence, vitality or peace.

In 1805, Little Harpe swung at the end of a rope for his crimes.

DIABOLIQUE
A Sibyl Novella

Their descendants changed their surname to distance themselves from the atrocities committed by the cousins. The luck of the damned, which protected them for so many years, disappeared that spring of 1799.

6. Dormant Evil

Henry gave Mrs. Manson the address of the cottage on Bourgoine Street. He warned her that only the direst circumstances should bring anyone seeking him there. The housekeeper bowed her head and kept quiet. She heard of persons who experienced a brush with death changing their ways, but she never saw it firsthand. She could swear another man sat in his place. A changeling had returned from the duel.

Pleading recovery from injuries, Henry left much of the work pending at the warehouse and the office in the hands of his partner Nicholas Semple. On the few days when he did come in to discuss business plans, Nicholas studied Henry with curious eyes. The bloating that once marred his jaw line and the puffiness under his eyes disappeared. He consumed less food and liquor, and his face thinned out as he lost weight. But, the most dramatic change concerned his business acumen, which always good, now became calculating and shrewd.

Semple wondered why Henry never brought up the subject of Noel Girod. The man he knew would have spoken incessantly of how to get revenge, through either another duel, or financial ruin. Girod made it obvious that he thought Beasley below his family's standards. His aim to kill Henry could not be mistaken as nothing else but disdain. The search for a bride also disappeared from topics of conversation.

Could it be due to the presence of a widow, newly arrived from Europe? Rumors circulated that Henry had set up house with this new mistress. Mysterious with her veiled face, she invited gossip from every quarter. Among the men bets were taken on her beauty; however, Semple remembered that Henry drew a strict line between business and pleasure. He could not think of a time where he saw him become sentimental towards another human.

Nicholas decided one day to test the waters of how unaffected Henry felt about the Girod affair. They were reviewing the manifest of the ship *New Hope*, which returned from a trip to Canton full of China goods, when he remarked, "Noel Girod might soon rob us of a ship's captain if what I hear is true."

Henry sat behind a large mahogany desk. He leaned back in his chair and raised a questioning brow at Semple, "Girod, again?"

"Yes, Captain Holbet and Natalie are seeing each other behind her family's back. The Girod family fears that one day Noel's luck will run out and he will be the one lying dead. He insists on challenging anyone that glances at Mademoiselle Natalie. To avoid further duels, I hear they are planning to ship her off to a convent in France, but in the meantime Girod has become an unlikeable fellow to be around."

DIABOLIQUE
A Sibyl Novella

"It makes one wonder if he is using his family's honor as an excuse to kill." Henry stated quietly.

Semple did not answer at once, for this subtle understanding of Girod's nature surprised him. "That has been commented upon, but our concern is that if he kills Holbet, we will have a ship full of goods without a captain. He is supposed to stop in Charleston on his way back to New York, and the word I have received is that several firms are eager to buy everything onboard. It will be a profitable trip for us."

Henry understood Nicholas' casual remarks better than he suspected. The time arrived to lay his suspicions to rest.

He smiled, but his eyes were serious. "Semple, we have known each other for many years, and you think I already planned retribution against Girod. I believe you were expecting me to rush off and meet him again to avenge my reputation. But those days I lay in bed nursing my wounds I gave thought how to crush Monsieur Girod."

"Beyond killing him?"

"If his sister were to run off with an American sea captain, the agony of this humiliation would be felt for years to come. Girod's pride will torture him until the day they bury him in St. Louis Cemetery."

Nicholas Semple eyed Henry with new respect and a tinge of fear. Manipulating the man's pride against him to embarrass him before society was a revenge that would cut a thousand times over.

"I want you to approach Holbet and assure him that if risks everything for sweet love, we will support him. He can elope with Mademoiselle Natalie, switch ships in Charleston and then make his way to New York. We will even give him a bonus to his salary, so he can set up home with his new wife. But this must come from you, for I believe I have fallen out of favor with Captain Holbet."

Semple nodded his head.

"Keep me informed of what goes on with this."

"As you wish."

Later that evening, Henry sent off his carriage to the house on Magazin Street and walked to the cottage on Bourgoine Street. A humid breeze stirred the branches overhead, and the light faded in the west. His walking stick made a slight noise as he meandered along the path. Overhead he could hear birds roosting, as they jostled one another for the same spot on a branch.

As he approached the house, he saw the stable boy Pepin, running up the street, casting quick glances over his shoulder. He vaulted over the gate in one leap. Breathing hard he stared in the opposite direction of where Henry stood. He then gave off a small scream and ran into the stable where Alegria whinnied at him.

Henry stopped and his eyes searched for what the boy ran from in such haste. The avenue appeared deserted, nothing moved in the gathering gloom of the fading daylight. Then he saw him, a man with a heavy coat, almost cape-like stumbling through the penumbra. He stared at the stables, where now a timid light shone from the window. The man wore a dark slouch hat covering his face. Over his shoulder, he carried a large, canvas bag.

"A peddler?" Henry wondered.

The man shuffled along and came to the edge of the gate leaning on a large staff he carried. Beyond it lay the field where Alegria grazed during the day, and towards the back stood the small stable.

Then he heard the low, raspy whisper coming from the figure, "Pepin, Pepin why do you run from me?"

It stood at the perimeter of the field, unable to go further, and then Ema knew a human would not be impeded, only a creature bound by the salt, prayers and other safeguards she had laid down once she took possession of the property. Henry watched as the figure kept calling the child's name.

Then from the gloom cast by the large tree hanging over the stables, a slim, wispy figure in white stepped forward timidly. It glided into the kitchen wall and dissolved. It resembled a teenage girl who by her actions feared what stood at the gate.

The large, bulky figure paced back and forth, hitting the gate with its staff. The darker the evening became, the louder it called. Henry observed it, mystified with the creature's insistence on calling Pepin out, until at last it said, "I am hungry, Pepin."

Then he understood the nature of the creature waiting impatiently. It consumed human flesh, but based on the little ghost's aversion to it, no doubt its true threat lay in its subsistence as a soul eater.

Henry made a noise with his walking cane and the figure turned around towards him. The face glowed milky white, with large staring eyes in a face absent of any expression. Its jaw hung unhinged, creating a mouth like a large cavern, something impossible for a human. It floated backwards into a growing patch of gloom and became absorbed by it. The dusk changed and the menace accompanying the figure dissipated.

Henry crossed the road and entered the home. A lamp on a small table cast a cozy luminescence, and he could smell delicious aromas coming from the kitchen in the back. He put aside his cane and mounted the stairs to the bedroom. He disrobed and lay on the bed. His body became limp, and then a violet light shimmered and outlined his form. Beside him, Ema's naked figure materialized. Her grayish blue skin held a moist sheen, which turned a rosy pink, her hair damp with droplets of water, started to dry instantly.

She slipped on a thin muslin gown, draped a shawl around her shoulders and went downstairs. The dining table lay set with one place, and a lantern stood lit close by. A window left ajar allowed nighttime sounds to drift in, along with an itinerant breeze. Ema sat at the table and sipped wine. She waited for her new cook to serve the evening's meal.

Isabel had knocked on the door several days ago, bearing a note from Blanche Beaupre. She immigrated to Cuba from Spain and then followed her husband, a soldier to New Orleans. He died several months ago. From one day to another, she found she did not have a way to keep a roof over her head. Blanche, who visited many households in her duties as a midwife, knew of her plight and steered her to the house on Burgoine Street.

Ema sat with her on the first day and explained her duties. She gave her access to a cash fund to be used to buy food and any other household expenses. To outward appearances, a pair of women sat in quiet conversation, but during their exchange Ema reached out to sense what type of person sat before her. Did darkness hide behind a sweet countenance or spiritual turbulence swirl around her? Ema only sensed a deep sadness at the death of her husband, and most profound her inability to conceive a child.

Ema took her to the kitchen, and then her quarters. That night Isabel lit a candle to the Virgin Mary in thanks for her good fortune. She embraced the added responsibility of caring for the stable boy and making sure he ate his meals. The child by his own choice, wished to keep sleeping in the stable with the horse.

Isabel was a middle-aged woman, thickening around the waist with kind brown eyes, and gray showing at her temple. She wore silver hoop earrings, and a red shawl. Merchants in the food stalls considered her one of their fiercest customers in securing the freshest food for the best prices.

That evening she served a steaming dish of rice and a recipe known as *Ropa Vieja*, made of shredded beef, vegetables and spices. She asked if Señor Henry wanted a tray prepared. Ema told her no. Then in a routine established within those first few days of her employment, she sat next to Ema and brought to her attention any matters of concern about running the house. Most importantly, she recounted the gossip that swirled in the neighborhood and the marketplace.

Isabel understood too well, that a servant became so much more valuable when they become a collector of information, in other words a spy. She admired the Madame's intelligence, because she knew the power of gossip. The true pulse of a city did not lie in the drawing rooms, but in the places where servants, slaves, soldiers and tradesmen lived and conducted business.

Isabel discussed the rumors running rampant that New Orleans would soon be under French rule. Ema smiled thinking politicians believed their machinations behind the scenes could stay secret. Then Isabel's face became serious, and she cleared her throat before speaking. She realized there was so little she knew about her mistress, but she suspected there were things she never wanted to know.

"Madame, I received a message for you."

"Who gave you this message?"

"Marie, she travels with her husband who is a peddler."

"Continue."

"Madame, everyone wonders what happened to Don Ambrosio Figueroa, but Marie assured me none at Belle Mer are sorry to see he has disappeared. I hope I don't offend you, but many people living there wish his body would be found in the river with a large stone tied around his neck."

"Yes, I heard that sentiment is common."

"Everyone knows you traveled with Don Ambrosio's brother who is a monk, and that you are now the owner of Belle Mer." Isabel stared at Ema, who kept eating without changing her expression. Isabel knew that her own status became elevated since she now served a woman, not only mistress to a wealthy merchant, but in her own right held dominion over a large sugar plantation.

Ema put aside her fork. She knew this conversation promised to be about more than who owned Belle Mer.

"Isabel, I do not own it. The King has asked me to oversee the running of it on behalf of the family. Certain disturbing facts have come to his attention. Brother Clemente with his vow of poverty has forfeited his rights of inheritance."

"Well then, Marie's message is meant for you. She said an old woman, well known in those parts, her name is Tante Ange asked that you to come to see her where she lives not too far from Belle Mer. She said something evil is stalking the plantation, and that the steward does not want to bring attention to it. He is not a bad man, but he fears losing his position or that you will blame him and dismiss him from his post."

"Yes I have heard of this woman. What else did Marie say?"

"Tante Ange came to live there as a young girl. She came as a slave, and bore children by the younger son of the Betancourt family who owned the plantation in those years. He freed her and their children and gave them a farm not too far away."

Ema commented, "I have heard she battled a demon that killed the slaves believed to be runaways."

"That is the story I have heard too." Isabel then crossed herself, before continuing, "The part that is never repeated because they could accuse one of heresy is..." Isabel paused, trying to gauge if Ema wanted her to continue.

"Have no fear Isabel; I will not accuse you of this. I know a true heretic when I see one, and they are not as common as the Church will have you believe."

"The demon disguised himself as a monk. No priest came to their aid. Even the Betancourt family started to suspect something unholy crept through the fields. In those years, they grew tobacco, and they saw that none of the slaves left the vicinity of the big house once the sun dipped into the west. Fires burned by the slave quarters throughout the night, and word came to them that even local Indian tribes were being ravaged."

"It sounds as if they were in a desperate situation." Ema commented.

"Yes, so they turned a blind eye when Tante Ange fought it with a magick she learned from her grandmother. She warned the family and the other slaves she could not vanquish it, she just sent it to a place where it could not continue to kill. Marie said this happened many years ago, and most have forgotten it."

"Then we will go to see Tante Ange."

"We?" Isabel stood with questioning eyes.

"In two days, you and Pepin will go with me."

DIABOLIQUE
A Sibyl Novella

The woman bobbed her head and wiped her hands on her apron. She left with hurried steps to make preparations.

Ema watched her retreating form. She dared not tell the woman she could not leave her or Pepin in the house without her protection. Based on Don Ambrosio's avoidance of the plantation Ema suspected that the creature Tante Ange battled so many years ago could be nothing else but a vampire. Now another evil arose, or perhaps the same diabolical thing banished so many years ago menaced Belle Mer once again.

7. Hell's Messenger

The next day dawned without a cloud in the sky, and Henry arrived early at his office. His box phaeton and two ponies were delivered to the house on Bourgoine Street. He informed Nicholas of his absence for a few days and asked him to handle any unforeseen personal matters on his behalf. Nicholas readily agreed wondering where his business partner was going, but prudently, he did not ask.

The following day, Pepin stood holding Alegria's reins, and Isabel sat in the phaeton. Inside the bedroom, Henry's body breathed deeply in its dreamless slumber.

They both stared in surprise when Ema came towards them for once not wearing a widow's veil. She wore a dark blue riding habit with a military cut, adorned with wide cuffs and gold buttons. Underneath she wore a dove gray chemisette. A straw hat tilted at a rakish slant on her head, and beneath it her red hair hid braided and coiled.

Pepin helped her mount, and he noticed the flintlock pistol and the long dagger held in a leather holster around her waist hidden by the jacket of her riding habit.

Isabel wondered how the short merchant secured this lovely Madame as his mistress. In a few months when summer passed and invitations for balls arrived, many Creole gentlemen would compete for her attention. Perhaps his dueling days were not over after all.

Ema smiled at them both, and Isabel and Pepin smiled back, both entranced by her green eyes. She had a thin face, with dark arched brows, over long-lashed sloe eyes. A generous mouth, naturally tinged a deep pink, offset the severity of her chiseled nose.

A mourning dove cooed in a nearby tree when Pepin took the reins and clucked to the ponies. With a jingle of harnesses, the group set off heading towards the outskirts of New Orleans.

A little after noon, Ema and her small entourage rode into a large farm, with children and chickens milling about under the shade of a large tree. She dismounted and a woman with a red tignon stepped from the verandah and welcomed her warmly. Hazel eyes offset her dark olive skin. She thanked her for coming to see her mother. She called for a servant to lead the animals to the stable. Another one took Isabel and Pepin to the kitchen so they could eat lunch.

She brought Ema to sit next to an old woman who sat in a rocking chair. A bright yellow tignon contrasted with her skin, the color of unsweetened chocolate. Her eyes sparkled like bits of jet amid the wrinkles surrounding them. Her daughter stepped away as Ema pulled off her gloves and settled in a comfortable chair next to the family matriarch.

DIABOLIQUE
A Sibyl Novella

The woman smiled and studied Ema. A servant brought a tray with tea, small sandwiches and pastries. Once they were alone, she spoke softly, "You came Madame, I knew you would."

"Tante Ange, your message intrigued me, and I am eager to hear what has caused such distress."

"Many years ago, I drove a great evil away from this place, but I am sure you have heard this story."

Ema nodded and waited for the woman to continue.

"The Betancourt family lost all their sons, including Hector the father of my children. Belle Mer became the property of one of their daughters who married a grandee in Spain, and for many years, they handled their affairs by proxy. Until one day, when her son Don Ambrosio Figueroa y Mujica came to claim Belle Mer."

Ema's face did not register any surprise, for she knew this. What occurred many years ago did not go unnoticed. When the first stories circulated in France and Spain about Don Ambrosio, they flamed the fears back to life.

Tante Ange nodded and continued, "I still have eyes and ears in Belle Mer, and this new master would not step outside until the sun disappeared. He wanted the curtains drawn, and the mirrors removed. One night he came to a place where I buried a powerful amulet in the earth. His skin started to smoke and his eyes bled. That night he left Belle Mer to New Orleans and did not return."

"And now?" Ema urged her.

The old woman clucked her tongue. She brought her finger to her eyes and said, "Where some see shadows, I see what is causing the shadow. It has always been so for me. I have seen him."

"Who have you seen?"

"The headless horseman, at the edge of the sugarcane fields, by the light of the full moon. He is a dark man riding a black horse, and he carries a head before him on the saddle."

"What does he want?"

"Nothing… now. He presages death. He is here before *le grand mal*, that awaits Lent. And it is because of you." She pointed with a forefinger that trembled.

"Me?" Ema asked with questioning eyes, but they held no surprise. Tante Ange studied her face. Now she understood. Despite the knowledge she had gained throughout her years of life, apprentice she had become once again.

"May I tell you a story Madame?" she asked Ema.

"Of course."

"When I banished the great evil that haunted Belle Mer, for years afterwards, none stayed in the fields once twilight started to fall. Even the steward and the overseer, made sure they were in proximity to the great house. All knew the only place safety could be found was there. Tales came to us of strange and perverted things taking trappers, hunters and runaway slaves who lived in the bayous. That is a treacherous

43

land to live in, so many shrugged their shoulders and dismissed the stories as superstition."

The old woman clucked her tongue again, "But you have driven Don Ambrosio away, he has fled from the city and forfeited his dominion over this piece of land. I could banish him, but you can destroy him. *Le rien*, nothing is here now, so another devil has come to take his place. This one is different, what I have laid down is crumbling. When the other one arrives, we will be at its mercy, as will those at Belle Mer."

Both women sat silent, a breeze flirting with the edges of their skirts. An afternoon sun beat down on the whitewashed walls of the farmhouse. Cicadas chirruped in the sugar cane fields that rustled beyond the vegetable garden. During this time of day most life becomes torpid, but under the golden light, the children of different ages came running as they played with a ball. Tante Ange pointed at Pepin, "It wants him."

Ema studied the boy, for once forgetting the hardships he endured in his short life as he ran and laughed with the other children. "Yes, I have seen something that chased him in the twilight."

"That child has not been promised to God, none have denounced Satan on his behalf."

"He is an orphan who found shelter through the kindness of strangers. He is now my stable boy. It is possible that he did not receive the sacrament of baptism."

"Then it is no accident that he comes to be in your care." Tante Ange observed.

"Listen to me Madame," the old woman said with urgency in her voice, "Ash Wednesday is in a few days, the time of sacrifice when Christians give up earthly pleasures, but there are other gods. Those who demand a sacrifice of human blood." She drew her finger across her neck in a sawing motion. "Starting with an innocent and I fear we will be at its mercy. Help us!"

"Tante Ange, I will help you, but you must try to protect yourselves as well."

"*Oui* Madame, again I thank you for coming to speak to me."

Ema and Tante Ange ate lunch. The day drifted on and they spoke of other things, ordinary life events, both women recognizing that time stopped for no one. When Ema gathered her small group to leave, the old woman pulled her aside once more.

"Promise me Madame you will tell no one it was I who drove away this demon that haunted these lands. It is already an old story, forgotten by most, but I know it is still there, restrained and hungering for blood. Its thirst has no end. I do not want my family destroyed because of what I did. I know you will outlive me, and all of us here, even that *bébé* carried in arms."

Ema nodded. She decided to return to New Orleans instead of going on to Belle Mer. Pepin and Isabel waited at the phaeton, and she mounted the mare being held by its rein. They waved their goodbyes and meandered down the narrow road that led onto the main one.

The silhouettes chased each other as the sun fell towards the western horizon. In the fading daylight they stopped to eat a quick meal of finger foods that Isabel had brought for them. They finished, and Pepin left to relieve himself behind a large tree trunk.

Isabel's frightened whisper called out to Ema, who stood next to the horse tightening the cinch on the saddle. "Madame, come quick."

Ema came to her side. She pointed to soft blue orbs of light that danced over a field. "Madame, you know what this is?" before Ema could answer, she continued, "The great house burned to nothing five years ago, many lost their lives and the place is cursed. This field is where they buried the members of the family for many years."

The words barely left her mouth, when they both heard Pepin's high-pitched wail of terror. Both women looked down the road and far away, they saw Pepin wrestling with a large, hulking shadow.

"Dios mio!" Isabel screamed, crossing herself.

The boy grappled with a hulking shadow that solidified into the same figure that Ema saw chasing him on Bourgoine Street. Tentacles snaked out to grab the boy who wrestled against it, as he tried to gain traction with his feet so he could run away. A bleached-bone face, with cavernous eyes and unhinged jaws turned to stare at Ema when she called out Pepin's name.

She heard Isabel whisper in horror, "The *Bonhomme Sept Heures*."

Despite the child's pretended hardness that he learned from living on the streets of New Orleans, when he wailed out "Madame" it sounded as the eternal cry of a child seeking protection.

Isabel heard Ema whisper something in a language she did not understand, and then she fell back when a turquoise light formed in Ema's hand, and a whip glowed in the evening light.

Isabel caught Ema's hat when she tore it off and threw it to her. Her long red hair became unbound. The crack of the whip traveled the length of the lonely road. Golden sparks outlined in aqua sparkled in the air, and the atmosphere grew electrified.

"Come." said Ema, in a voice echoing like the peal of a glass bell. She pointed her finger towards her side.

The hulking figure stared for a moment and tried harder to pull the child under his arm and throw him inside a large sack it carried on its back. Pepin's eyes bugged out, and he struggled more than ever, knowing that once inside it no one could help him. Somewhere far afield a lone wolf howled.

Ema thought in alarm, "Did he ignore my command?"

She stripped off her outer jacket, and then time appeared to stand still, and every sound evaporated, distance as well became irrelevant. Isabel stared with her mouth agape from under the phaeton where she crouched. One moment Ema's body stood beside her and then in the blink of an eye she stood next to the dark figure and the struggling child.

Ema grabbed the thing's wrist where it held Pepin by his upper arm. It dropped the child who fell to the ground with a thud. The arm became a tentacle that wrapped around Ema's waist. The thing's face resembling a bearded man, transformed into something barely human. Out of the cavern of its mouth, more tentacles disgorged, and the two eyes became milky white, and a third, red-rimmed eye opened in its forehead. Out of the end of the tentacle holding Ema a mouth full of long, sharp teeth erupted.

The figure grew larger, letting out a long, thunderous growl. It lifted Ema off the ground. A harsh wind came out of nowhere whipping down the road that grew in obscurity as the sun set in the west. Another howl sounded, but closer now.

Pepin scampered back to where the phaeton stood, and he grabbed Alegria's reins holding the horse as it stamped its hooves and looked around with startled eyes. From the field full of tilting tombstone grunts and cries rang out, like wretched souls in agony.

"Is that the best you can do?" Ema asked the thing before using the butt of the whip to strike the eye that blinked in its forehead. Ema's skin turned a bright pink and the smell of burning flesh filled the air. The thing screamed in agony as the suckers on the tentacle blackened, and it unfurled from around Ema's waist.

The air sizzled when the lash arced through the space leaving behind an aqua line that shimmered before disappearing.

"What do you want?" the woman asked in a voice that crackled.

The tentacles stretched out and pointed to Pepin, "The child."

"You cannot have him, I claim him."

The thing howled, the tentacles inside its mouth writhing and flailing about in fury. The urchin found a protector, and he could not take him unless he defeated the woman that caused it such pain by only touching her skin.

Down the embankment from the road lay an overgrown field. Something moved, catching Ema's eyes. A figure mounted on a steed watched her. The animal's eyes were red embers, and puffs of vapor smoked from its nostrils. It existed in an eternal winter with its rider, a cloaked figure draped in black. On the horn of the saddle sat a human head, mouth agape in everlasting astonishment that it was cleaved from the body.

In that moment, she knew she could not leave Isabel and Pepin unguarded. She snapped the whip and as the tip hit the earth she said, *"Custos nigrum."* The ground split open and a hiss of steam shot upwards. Something scratched then pushed its way out. First a long snout, then forepaws pushed until the rest of the body emerged. A large shaggy, black dog that dwarfed the size of a pony stood immobile.

Ema sent a mental message to Pepin instead of Isabel, calculating that he could understand what she wanted. She knew he had learned to master fear and survive. Her thought shot towards him like an arrow, "Do not fear, cover their eyes."

She saw the child's eyes widen, and he nodded imperceptibly. She turned to the black dog that lay at her feet, its red eyes full of licking flames. "Guard them," and she showed with her whip where her two servants stood.

The animal stood and loped towards them. Pepin took off his short coat and threw it over Alegria's eyes, and he told Isabel to do the same to the ponies. She tore off her shawl and with trembling hands covered their heads.

The dog came to stand next to them, and then it raised it hackles and let out a howl, claiming its stake next to the humans. The horse and ponies stamped their feet and whinnied but stayed in place, tugging on their reins.

Night fell, and Ema saw the red dancing lights burning inside the Grim's eyes. From a canopy of branches overhead, one leaf fell, glowing with a neon purple color. When it touched her head, it moved of its own accord, attaching itself to the end of her braid.

Ema cracked the whip, and her voice sounded like the wind, "Take him if you can."

The road lit up in the thrumming glow of the whip, and her eyes glimmered with the same aquamarine light.

The Bonhomme Sept Heures studied her. This creature preyed on disobedient or careless children, or like Pepin those orphaned of a protector. It disguised itself as a bearded man; a mendicant that carried a sack over one shoulder, which many guessed contained only scraps and junk, never suspecting what lay stuffed inside its infinite depths.

Ema knew it could not withdraw now. A mournful laughter came from its razored mouth; a hollow, distant sound devoid of humor. Suddenly a tentacle shot out from its midsection, grabbed Ema by the ankle and jerked her off her feet. The stink of rotted flesh drifted out from it, as it pulled her roughly towards him. She slapped the whip against her palm and it hardened, lengthened and became a staff. From her prostate position, she swung it hard across its face, and black, putrid liquid misted across her. Its grip on her ankle released, and she then swung the staff underneath it and it toppled forward. She regained her feet and moved away.

Ema knew you couldn't kill something, which had never been alive. This thing could only be true to its nature. Created within the disorder of chaos, it counterbalanced Divine Order, and she could not spend eternity trading blows with it.

She twirled the staff in her hand in a motion that blurred. When she stopped, she held a bow and a quiver of arrows. She nocked one arrow and blew against the fletching. A quivering silver rope materialized and attached to it. She let it fly, and it impaled the Bonhomme square in its chest, since by now it had regained its feet. The rope like a thing alive wound various times around the creature immobilizing it from any other movement. The cord glowed in the road's darkness.

Ema approached it. The Bonhomme snuffled and roiled against the ropes.

"Get rid of those tentacles and speak to me," she commanded it.

As if by magic, the tentacles moved back inside the orifice and a leering, misshapen mouth formed.

"Do you accept defeat?" Ema asked it in a steady voice.

"Great Sibyllina, if I knew the boy belonged to you, I would never have sought to take him."

"But you tried to take him, not once but twice. I will ask once more. Do you accept defeat?"

"Yes." A gurgled voice answered.

"I will release you, but I will state the conditions under which I grant you freedom. If you ever try to take the boy again, or any child that lives on the farm I just visited or the Belle Mer plantation I will see it as an attack on my person."

The milky eyes became unfocused but the third eye in its forehead squinted in resistance.

In less time than it takes to draw breath, Ema's eyes blazed with lightning, and she glowed a deep blue that turned white. Her voice growled deeper and more ominous than any animals that hunted in the forest, and it reverberated down the lonely avenue. She grabbed the Bonhomme by its neck and lifted it up into the air.

"You do not realize the gift I give you. I believe you are taking too long to consider your answer; for I can easily believe you have declared war on me, and this will give me the right to drag you off to the Place of No Shadows; only light, eternal and unrelenting."

"Sibyllina, mercy, mercy on one you have defeated." The thing croaked.

Ema threw it to the ground. "Consider yourself warned."

She waved her hand, and the rope dissolved and released the black, lumpy figure. She clapped once, the figure lost its solidity and disintegrated in a cloud of dark ashes that were carried away by the wind.

The headless figure watching from the edge of the field faded, and the howling stopped. Only the call of insects and the rustling of animals moving through the underbrush filled the night.

Ema wandered in the darkness to where her jacket lay on the ground. She snapped her fingers and opened a small circle in the air in front of her. Her weapons disappeared into the circle that closed with a pop, became a small cube and then sank into her outstretched palm. She then fell to her knees and started to dry heave, followed by vomit. Her gut wrenched inside her torso. The Grim padded up to her, sat on its haunches and waited.

"Thank you, I am in your debt." She mumbled after she sat back on her heels, wiping her mouth. It stood up and sauntered off into the darkness, dissolving into the waving stalks of sugarcane.

Further up the road she heard Isabel's uncertain voice, "Madame, do you need our help?"

"No, no, just give me a moment." Ema felt the world twirl around her when she tried to stand up straight. She thought, "What better time to remember religious sayings than when you are spilling the contents of your stomach on a lonely country road?" Like a dutiful child accepting their well-deserved punishment, her mind berated her with the words she knew were true, "'Pride goeth before destruction, and a haughty spirit before a fall.' You can call on her, she is but syllables away."

Ema said aloud to no one except herself, "No!"

48

It took a few minutes, and she stood on wobbly legs. She inhaled deeply and shuffled down the road. Once the glow of the lantern on the phaeton illuminated her, Pepin ran towards her and then wrapped his arms around her, whispering, "My Madame, you saved me." She stumbled, feeling her balance teeter.

Ema hugged the child back and then took his hand as they meandered back to where Isabel waited. The cook stood by the phaeton with large, round eyes. Fear pinched her face.

"I can make you forget what you saw, and then you will not carry the burden of keeping the secret you are now a part of for the rest of your life. What is your answer?" Ema offered her.

"It is no burden Madame, of the fear that entered my heart; you and Pepin under threat of that monster squeezed my heart with terror." She approached Ema and took her hand, "You look so pale."

The woman touched Ema's forehead and cheek. Her skin felt clammy, "You have my word I will keep my silence. There is much I don't understand, but I know that you saved this boy."

Isabel turned to Pepin, "Tie Alegria to the back, and come help Madame to sit up here next to me."

"Then let us go home." Ema said in a tired voice.

Isabel perched the lantern on a hook next to her and took the reins. Pepin sat between both women, and a few minutes later the child snuggled against Ema and fell asleep. The clop of hooves and the squeak of the carriage's wheels filled the night's silence.

8. Sacrifices

Hours later when they arrived at the house on Bourgoine Street, Pepin roused himself and took care of the animals

Once inside her room Ema slipped inside of Henry's form. He stood up, stretched his muscles and went to relieve himself. He stared at the deserted street below the window.

Inside the man's form, Ema realized that even now she knew her full strength evaded her, and therefore access to all her powers. She had learned a hard lesson of what happened when she joined with avatars or "pockets" which held onto life by a thread. They were more susceptible to disease, especially if they suffered from an illness or physical impairment beforehand. Now with Henry Beasley she only enjoyed a respite before having to find a new avatar, and a sentient one could only be chosen by following a strict protocol. The first, most important caveat in this exchange was that the person faced certain death.

This time she had taxed herself to a dangerous level. Questions chased one another inside her mind, "What if she could not summon the strength to rejoin Henry's body? What if the only weapon she could have wielded against the Bonhomme Sept Heures was vomit?"

The next morning, Henry sat at the breakfast table. Isabel hovered around him and asked if she should prepare a tray for Madame. He told her no, that she rested in the bedroom. His eyes scanned the newspaper *Moniteur de la Louisiane* and his attention went to a short article.

TWO WOMEN BURNED TO DEATH
New Orleans, February 3, 1799
A terrible casualty occurred here at an early hour this morning resulting in the loss of two lives. A little frame shanty on 16th street took fire. The flames spread so rapidly as to get beyond control. Before the fire burst forth it had been smoldering for some time and partially suffocated the inmates. The house fell in and two women Julia Therkles aged 36, and her daughter, aged 14 were burned to death. The elder woman's body when found was minus the limbs, and her daughter's body was minus the head.

If Ema ever entertained doubts whether Don Ambrosio left New Orleans, they were gone. Vampires, like other hellish creatures staked out a territory. His absence signaled to others they could come to plunder what he once claimed as his own. These two women which were dismembered, with a fire set as a clumsy effort to hide the true cause of their death, pointed to a new predator claiming New Orleans as their hunting ground. His eyes scanned further on the page and he read confirmation of this suspicion.

50

A WOMAN'S BODY
Found Dead in the Swamp in Rear of the City.

Yesterday evening at about 5:30 o'clock the body of a servant woman named Maria Jaramillo was found about one square from Toulouse Street. The woman left her house on Canal Street, last Saturday with her tin bucket, evidently to go blackberrying. Her failure to return seemed to cause no alarm until yesterday when the police were notified of her absence. Last evening a char girl named Guillermina Garcia, while picking blackberries found the body near the bush, and immediately gave the alarm. The body is very much decomposed and a portion of the face has been eaten away. There were no marks of violence on the body, and the authorities are puzzled what precipitated her death.

Ema realized more than ever, that she did not have what she needed the most, which was time. On one hand she had a pocket with a precarious hold on his health, and on the other she had unknown enemies that could force her into a confrontation at any moment.

Later that afternoon, Henry met with Nicholas Semple at the warehouse to inspect goods due to leave on the ship *Venus* in two days bound for New York. Her captain Andrew Coffin met with them to make sure everything was in order. Henry charged him to deliver a special mail packet to his solicitors in the city. Unknown to any but him he instructed that his home and warehouse in New York be sold. He knew he would never return there.

While they were there, Nicholas pulled Henry aside. "I spoke to Captain Holbet as you asked. He knows the Girod family will never accept him, and he is trying to convince Mademoiselle Natalie that she will have to leave them behind if they are ever to be together. He said that once she leaves the city for the summer and goes to their plantation, he will never see her again."

Henry studied Nicholas with a calculating eye. "Tell Holbet he better hurry on the convincing part because we cannot afford to keep him here for a few months. Tell him to kidnap her if he has to."

"Henry, this will cause a scandal. It will ruin her reputation, and her family will disown her."

"Perhaps this is what she waits for all along. It will ease her conscious towards her family if she's forced to leave. As to being ousted from her family's good graces that is inevitable. Holbet needs to find out if she loves him as she professes to do."

Semple raised a disapproving brow, but then muttered, "Henry I didn't realize you understand human nature so well, and I hate to admit it, but you are probably right."

"I know I am." That ended the conversation.

Henry went to his home on Magazin Street. He called Mrs. Manson to his study. The woman sat uneasily on the edge of her chair and eyed him warily. He appeared the same, but disturbingly different, and she couldn't quite place her finger on it.

"Mrs. Manson, you have been a dutiful housekeeper, but I will come to the point. I will move away from this house and be putting it on the market. I want you to dismiss the staff except for two who can stay behind to put it in order along with you. Tell them they will receive two weeks wages and a letter of reference. You and your helpers can stay until the end of February, and I will give each one of you a month's wage and good references."

The woman gasped and glanced at him with disbelieving eyes. Could this be due to his new mistress? Keeping a second household for a liaison was a common arrangement, but these relationships existed out of the public eye. She nodded her head, and whispered, "As you wish Mr. Beasley, I will attend to it."

"I have an associate by the name of John Blanque. His housekeeper has grown elderly and infirm, and he's mentioned that he is seeking to replace her. The household is just him and his wife. Would you be interested in this position? I could mention your name."

Her eyes lit up, and she said yes and thanked him.

Henry knew that the job belonged to her, but he would go through the formalities. John Blanque owed him a tremendous debt. His favorite whore took an overdose of laudanum when he told her he would not be returning to seek her services any longer. She waited until he fell asleep in her bed, and he woke to find her gasping for breath next to him. Henry happened to be visiting the same brothel and procured a physician who attended the woman, and saved her because of his prompt intervention. He snuck John out through a rear door. Henry got the distinct impression the madam delayed in getting help so her employee would die, and she could blackmail John Blanque.

Once Mrs. Manson left, Henry studied everything around him. He prided himself on his expensive tastes. The rugs under his feet were oriental and the walnut furniture of the finest quality. Porcelain figurines graced the mantelpiece. Ema realized that despite his wealth and enjoying the finer things in life, her avatar did not achieve happiness.

He gathered more clothing and filled a trunk with instructions to have it delivered to the house on Bourgoine Street. He returned to the small cottage, and a short time later Ema came down the stairs to eat in the dining room. Isabel came to sit next to her. The brief conversation ended when Ema reminded her she could never speak of what she saw, she then gave her special instructions to buy clothing for Pepin.

Then she asked the cook a question, "Isabel would you stand as Pepin's godmother?"

"His godmother, his *madrina*?"

"I am not sure, but I believe Pepin has never been baptized. You saw what tried to take him."

"Yes, if he is not baptized, he cannot enter heaven. I will be his godmother, but who will be his godfather?"

"Mr. Beasley."

Isabel said nothing, because accepting the responsibility as a godparent demanded an obligation towards the child, and seldom did a wealthy merchant do this for an orphan.

Ema said, "It will take place on Ash Wednesday."

"Tomorrow is Mardi Gras, will you not be attending the ball? It is a grand affair, and there will be no festivities until Easter."

"Henry is not ready to attend. I do not want him to meet Noel Girod, which undoubtedly will occur at this ball."

"I can understand that there is still bad blood between them. M'sieur Girod has a reputation for winning duels, and many tears have been shed because of him. He always aims to kill his opponent." The woman nodded at Ema. "You are wise Madame, very wise."

Early the next morning Ema rode out to St. Louis Cathedral. She met with Père Antoine and he agreed to baptize Pepin. When she told him who the godparents were to be, he hid his surprise, but he could not disguise his disbelief when Ema told him she wanted Pepin to attend school. Capuchin monks instructed boys in reading, writing, music and religion, but stable boys were usually not among the students.

Ema smiled at him, and then remarked, "There are so many finishing touches the cathedral needs after being rebuilt. I know you would like to have a new clock and bell. Perhaps part of the funds needed for this work is the loaf of bread that Pepin will bring under his arm for St. Louis."

Père Antoine nodded, understanding too well what she meant, but he could not help but wonder if this child held special abilities. Madame Duplessis made it obvious the mantle of her protection lay over him.

Ema departed and once outside made her way toward where the same boy held Alegria's reins. She then heard the slap-slap of sandals coming up behind her. She turned and found Brother Clemente striding towards her with an intense expression on his face.

"Madame Duplessis, please stop."

Brother Clemente saw she no longer wore the dark veil over her face. Even though he glimpsed her many times throughout their voyage, her beauty hypnotized him. The sun danced on wisps of reddish hair that escaped the hat she wore.

Jealousy churned in his gut. He heard rumors that a wealthy protector claimed her and gave her a place to live. He wondered if this liaison existed before she left Europe. What he would have given to paint her as the Madonna, or perhaps an angel, and then bring her to his bed.

He could not speak to her of this, so he used a safer subject.

"My brother, have you seen him? I have tried to find where he is at so I may speak to him. Only now am I learning of his grim reputation. Many are surprised to find that he has a brother who took holy orders."

"No Brother Clemente, I have not, and word has reached me he might have left the city. Where he has gone is unknown."

"I must find him," the monk muttered, "I must hear it from his lips why these things are said about him, and if there is any truth that he had a hand in our family's murder."

"Brother Clemente, I wish I could set your mind at ease but I understand that your brother's reputation is well-earned. Perhaps you should wait and see if he reaches out to you."

"My brother is no saint, but many things hinted at make me fear for his soul. I believe Ambrosio might be in the devil's grip. I must save him if I can."

Ema knew that despite Brother Clemente's suspicions, she doubted he could face the horror of what stained his family's name.

"Then patience is the only choice. I cannot help but tell you to be cautious in meeting him. If he is in the grip of something that does not understand filial love and loyalty a meeting could be dangerous. Now, I must leave, since other duties demand my attention."

Brother Clemente stared at her with yearning. He made the sign of the cross over her in blessing and murmured, "I understand."

Ema strode to where her horse waited, mounted with ease and rode off among the people of New Orleans who prepared for Mardi Gras festivities. A queer sense of heightened celebration stirred among the populace. They realized the new century ended in a few months, and this carnival held special significance. She knew many aberrations in human behavior would be blamed on carnivalesque madness. but, she could not afford to enter the spirit of abandon. Ema understood that this transition from one century to another in reality meant nothing.

9. The Dispossessed

Riders and carriages passed next to Ema as she rode down the Vieux Carre, but her thoughts took her far from this place. Part of her pitied Brother Clemente for various reasons, but she could not afford to forget he acted as a spy for the Vatican. They tasked him to watch her and report on her movements. No doubt by now he wrote missives to them about what happened on the *San Amaro*. They did not tell him the reason for their scrutiny, but his loyalty to the Church, assured his obedience.

Her own message would soon be wending its way back to Europe. The recipients were a secret sect within the Vatican known as the Sempiterno Apostasy. The members were only a handful of people who understood the truth of her nature. They infiltrated the Vatican because stories of unearthly and evil creatures were acknowledged and catalogued there.

Their members comprised a select few. Once a human being became possessed by an evil entity, in almost every circumstance, the forceful ejection of this spirit from their "pocket", through exorcism or other mystical means, spelled death for the human host. Only a few survived the trauma. Shattered in mind and body, they were a drooling and shivering visage of their former selves.

Even rarer still, were those who survived, traumatized and scarred, but intact. Collectively they were known as the "Dispossessed". The extent these humans remembered or buried their experience varied, but each were marked for their entire lives. This spiritual blemish represented a terrible curse to some, and an enlightening gift to others. The minds of the Dispossessed were open to the world beyond. They were able to see its inhabitants, and in turn be seen by them. Experiences suffered by the former 'possessing' spirit troubled them in times of stress or doubt. They were held hostage by old memories, but also by flashes of things yet to come.

Some embraced the curse enriching themselves; others sought answers to ever-deeper mysteries. Yet many railed against it, leading solitary and secluded lives, fearing the World Beyond. These few who survived physically, spiritually and mentally were inducted into the Sempiterno Apostasy. Who comprised this sect became one of the most sought after secrets in the Vatican. Even the most powerful cardinals and the Inquisition feared them.

In the fall of 1798, chill winds chased leaves through the streets of Paris, when Ema rode out to the countryside to a secret location where messages arrived via homing pigeons. Few knew they could reach her this way. When a gray, cooing pigeon with a message for Columba awaited her, the short missive from Sister Clare put her on the road that very day heading to Madrid.

Ema was surprised when Sister Clare found her years after they parted ways. It seemed that the nun acted as an emissary for the Sempiterno Apostasy. Their friendship had been forged during those days when she still lived in Paris. Sister Clare received word arrests warrants had been issued for her family since they were aristocrats. In her desperation, she turned to Madame Duplessis, as she knew her then, for help in saving them. Ema smuggled them out of France only hours before a mob marched on their chalet. In turn, Sister Clare covered her movements while they both lived behind the walls of the Madelonnettes Convent

Ema was later to learn the reason the Sempiterno Apostasy sought her out. Despite their extensive reach in the Old World, in the New World they were woefully ignorant. Dark beings "pocketed" humans who willingly gave themselves over to them in return for riches, titles and dominion over other humans. They mingled with the waves of humanity that came to these foreign shores. From stories detailed by explorers for the last three hundred years, there were entities only found in these unexplored lands.

However, their request remained secret; the acknowledged reason for her voyage to New Orleans was to find Don Ambrosio Figueroa y Mujica.

Memories faded, and Ema patted Alegria's neck, urging her to a canter. She headed to a secret location where a message would start its trip to the Sempiterno Apostasy. Its contents were simple: *Don Ambrosio, family annihilator and vampire fled New Orleans to parts unknown; but other dark beings roam the Louisiana Territory claiming humans in body and spirit. I do not plan to return.*

10. Dark of the Moon

Ema stood at the window of her room. Candlelight made shadows dance against the walls. She could hear the far off sound of music and revelry, which drifted in along with the cool February air. Time enough to repent tomorrow on Ash Wednesday, when sins whispered in the confessional, would be negotiated for penitence and forgiveness. The moonless night stirred with many things in its inky penumbra, most of them inhuman.

Ema lay next to Henry's prostrate form, and her nude body shimmered and then dissolved. The hours passed. A heart-shaped pendulum swung in an ornate narrow clock at the foot of the stairs, and it rang three times. The silence ended, interrupted by a knock on the entrance door of the cottage. Desperation could be sensed in the repeated rat-tat-tat.

By the time, Ema descended the stairs Isabel met her there. The cook draped a shawl around her long nightgown, and her hair straggled in disheveled strands around her face. She stared at Ema with questioning eyes.

Then a man's voice, low but urgent sounded through the door, "Beasley for the love of God, open the door."

Isabel queried through the closed door, "Sir who are you?"

One could hear the relief in the man's voice when he answered. "Tell Señor Beasley, Captain Holbet calls on him regarding an urgent matter."

Ema unbolted the door, and a tall man practically fell into the room. He dragged a woman behind him, his hand clamped around her wrist. His eyes swung around the room searching for Henry and settled on Ema. Next to him stood a woman wearing a costume with a tear-stained face. Her white wig tilted askew, and in her other hand she held a carnival mask.

"Forgive this intrusion, but Mr. Beasley's housekeeper directed me here to find him."

Ema answered in a quiet voice, "He is not here, Captain Holbet."

Desperation sprung on the man's face. Ema could see he warred whether to ask her if she knew where her paramour celebrated Mardi Gras. As Henry's mistress, in exchange for his support and protection, she agreed to accept that he could pursue his pleasures wherever he wished.

"Captain Holbet, I see something untoward has happened. I may help. This lady, she is distraught. Come my dear, sit a moment."

Ema could see the man weighing whether to discuss his dilemma with her. He thought she had no knowledge of his predicament.

"Isabel, take this mademoiselle to the dining room and bring her a tisane."

The woman glanced at Ema with grateful eyes and nodded her head. She followed Isabel out of the room.

Ema said, "Captain Holbet, I will come to the point. Henry has confided to me about your dilemma. Am I right to assume this is Natalie Girod?"

The man's eyes widened in surprise, "Yes." he answered uncertainly.

"You have knocked on the front door of this cottage because circumstances forced you. Please put aside any distaste or caution you have in speaking to me, as a woman and Henry's mistress. I might help you more than you suspect."

The man sighed and plunged into his story. "Madame I am the captain of a ship owned by Mr. Beasley. I fell in love with Mademoiselle Girod and she returned my affection, but her family forbade our relationship. Her family is proud, and this led to the duel between her brother and Mr. Beasley. I received word through Nicholas Semple, that Beasley extended help to us if we ever eloped. I bargained to have more time to convince Natalie of this plan."

The man paused, and Ema questioned, "But you became aware of something?"

"Yes, at a tavern only a few days ago I sat conversing with Lieutenant Lazard from the French schooner *L'Epine*. He commented on the hefty purse the captain received to transport a special passenger, a certain Natalie Girod, back to France. He assumed a convent in France awaited her, no doubt to quiet wagging tongues and deter a scandal. Her brother Noel made special inquiries which ship was the first one to sail after Mardi Gras."

"I see," interrupted Ema, "so her brother intended to ship her in secret to France?"

"Yes, I know he feared Natalie might agree to become my wife in secret. Once that ship sailed there would be no hope of finding her."

"But she appears distraught Captain Holbet; does she wish to go with you?"

"Yes she does, but her brother has a powerful hold on her. Her father passed away, and her mother lost another daughter only a few years ago. They often remind Natalie she cannot cause any more grief to her mother's heart. He does not take into account his sister's happiness, so I took her from the ball. Even now I am sure her brother is scouring the city searching for us."

"Captain Holbet, Henry left a message for you. If you will wait for me a moment I will bring it to you."

"Yes, of course."

Once inside the bedroom, Ema wrote a note in Henry's handwriting. It instructed Captain Coffin to allow William Holbet and Natalie onboard, and to take them in secrecy to New York. She sealed the letter in wax with Henry's ring and brought it to the man who paced as he waited for her.

"Take this letter to Captain Andrew Coffin. His ship is the *Venus*, and it will sail in two days time."

"Yes, I know him." No sooner did the words leave his mouth, than a loud woman's scream came from the dining room accompanied by the sound of breaking china.

Ema, Captain Holbet and Isabel rushed to Natalie's side.

DIABOLIQUE
A Sibyl Novella

"I saw her!" Natalie wailed. "Mon Dieu! Celeste, she stood there in the doorway."

"Who did you see?" Captain Holbet caught her by the shoulder.

Natalie's face filled with terror. "My sister, Celeste."

"But you told me she is dead."

"Yes, yes, Nicholas told us. He did not want to cause us pain with the details, and just said the devil took her. But, I saw her now dressed in a stained and ripped gown. Her face appeared pale and unhappy."

Captain Holbet took Natalie in his arms, "You are distraught my dear."

"But I tell you, I saw her. And this house, there is something familiar about it, but I cannot recall why."

Ema stepped towards the pair. "Captain Holbet, I suggest you leave now and speak to Captain Coffin. Leave Natalie here with me, and we will find a change of clothing for her. Her brother is searching for a woman dressed in costume."

The man nodded understanding the need for secrecy.

"But I will insist on the following instructions. Stay and wait for us on the ship. I will take Natalie to the docks."

"Madame, this plan is foolhardy; the wharves are no place for ladies."

"You are right, but these circumstances demand it. Monsieur Girod will have many eyes seeking a man fitting your description. We must throw them off your trail. Do you have anyone onboard your ship that you can trust will not betray you?"

Captain Holbet searched Ema's eyes, wondering at her question. "Yes, I do."

"I want you to have this person waiting with a green scarf around his neck. He can row Natalie out to the *Venus*."

Ema saw Captain Holbet found himself in a quandary. He did not want to leave Natalie behind, but he understood the wisdom of Ema's explanation.

"Captain, once the sun rises, it will be much easier to find you both. Noel Girod will never suspect you and Natalie are onboard the *Venus*. You have both taken a great risk, do not waste this opportunity."

Holbet nodded, knowing this gamble had to be played out despite any risks. Ema glanced at Natalie who appeared to be in a daze. The captain took her by the shoulders, kissed her on the forehead and marched from the room. Isabel locked the door when he left.

Ema stepped up to Natalie and touched her lightly between the eyebrows. Natalie's eyes drooped, and her features became expressionless. Ema studied her. She must be in her late twenties, long past marriageable age among Creole society. Her heart-shaped face framed by luxurious brown hair and her dark eyes could easily ensnare a man's heart. This coupled with her family's wealth; no doubt brought various suitors seeking her hand. Why had her brother kept her from marriage?

Ema whispered to Natalie, "You will obey me in everything I say. The sound of my voice will soothe you and fear will leave you now. Answer me; do you love Captain Holbet?"

"Yes, very much." She said in a monotone voice.

"Do you wish to be his wife and escape with him to New York?"

"Yes, with all my heart."

"Why has your brother refused the marriage offers made for you?"

"I don't know. I do not understand why he is so cruel even though he says he loves me. He says he is carrying out our father's wishes, and that our family's name must be honored at all costs. He says I must resign myself to caring for our mother and him since he has no wife. Sometimes I am afraid of him."

Isabel came back to the room, and Ema instructed her to dress Natalie in servant's clothing. Isabel led the woman back to her quarters.

Ema went upstairs and pulled out a set of men's clothing that she paid to have tailored for her. They were plain, a coat with high lapels, narrow trousers and boots. All were black, including a waistcoat and a silk cravat. She coiled her braided hair at the back of her neck.

On the bed, Henry Beasley's body breathed, but no expression animated his face.

Ema rubbed her hands together, causing a frisson in the air. She blew into her hands and said, "Come spirit, now that I know your name. Come Celeste Girod."

Out of a dark wedge in the corner, a pale figure shimmered and then coalesced. A woman glided forward. Long dark hair hung around her face, and she wore a white dress torn and full of stains. She bore a similarity to Natalie, but dark circles surrounded her eyes and her cheeks were sunken. A cadaver stood there.

"Speak now Celeste, for I can hear what you have to say."

Her voice sounded remote and unused. Her mouth did not move, but her words were clear in Ema's mind, and as she spoke the scene unfolded as seen through Celeste's eyes.

"Natalie, I love her so. Save her."

"I will help her, but you are not bound here because of her."

"Only a fool dismisses her sister's warning. She told me Nicholas would never let me escape and taint the family's honor. I did not heed her. I did not think my brother hated me so he would murder me for the crime of falling in love."

Ema asked her, "Who did you love?"

"The youngest son of the Vicomte de Nogent sought my hand, and my brother refused. His family is an old and noble one, and I could not understand why he did this. He told those who asked that my youth prevented him from giving his consent. Nevertheless, my lover sent me letters, asking me to join him on his plantation in Martinique as his wife. I ran away and stayed here where my old nurse lived. I awaited a ship soon to arrive with instructions to take me to him. Summer came and everyone fled the city as the fever claimed both old and young. My nurse Bosette hid me, but my brother knew where to find me."

The wraith continued in a monotone voice, devoid of any emotion.

DIABOLIQUE
A Sibyl Novella

"He strangled me and buried me under a kettle used to boil soap behind this house. He did the same to Bosette, but he left her body here in this room. They did not discover her for many days. Old and infirm, they thought she died of the fever. He sent my lover a letter saying I died from the fever, and to every other person who asked he told the same story. My grave next to my father is empty."

"Is this why you have no peace?" Ema asked her with a knowing expression on her face.

"No, after my brother killed me, he dug a hole to bury me. Even though my body lay lifeless on the ground, he told me a story as if he knew I could hear his words. A terrible understanding came to me then, when I had no power to change the outcome of what I had done."

"And what did he say?"

"That my mother told him to kill me."

"Now that you know more than your brother does, why did she do this?"

"As a young girl she fell in love with an unsuitable man known to be debauched and a seducer of young women. Her family refused the match and promised her to my father. His family he lost to sickness years before, but he still yearned to have other children and a loving wife. He was a good man, but loneliness blinded him. My mother's bitterness knew no bounds, and she purposefully gave herself to a half-wit who worked in the stables. When she wed my father, she already carried my brother in her belly. Foolishly, he only knew joy that she produced a child so quickly, but my mother hated my father. Natalie and I are both his children, and she determined that none of his bloodline should survive. She condemned us to childlessness. Her offspring with a servant, stood to inherit his entire fortune. She started to poison my father soon after Celeste's birth, but she did it slowly so it appeared he died from a wasting sickness. My brother, she showered with love, and her daughters she treated with disdain. She tutored him in hate. He does not know the truth of who beget him."

"Wouldn't your father's fortune go to Noel since he is the eldest and the only male offspring?" Ema asked her.

"No, my father specified in his will that his daughters should each inherit a portion of his fortune upon our marriage. Only Marysas would go in its entirety to Noel. These conditions were kept secret. This is the reason no suitor found approval with him, but he could not afford another sister to die, because already many in our circle commented on his strange refusal to see his sisters married. Suspicion stirred in the minds of many, including my father's family. The Girod many times offered to bring us to live with them, but my mother turned them away. She planned that Natalie should end her days in a cloistered convent where the sisters take a vow of silence, but my father's family would learn of her whereabouts after she had left."

"What will your brother do if he finds her now?" Ema asked.

"He will kill her."

"Celeste, what will ease your spirit?"

"Save my sister, and lay my bones next to my father, who loved me and Natalie."

"Celeste I will try, but in the meantime do not scare my stable boy or the cook."

The specter bowed her head, stepped back into the corner, and faded into the darkness.

Isabel waited downstairs with Natalie, now dressed in a plain gown with a mantilla draped over her head. Ema instructed Isabel her not to open the door to anyone, whatever the reason they gave. Isabel's eyes widened when she saw Ema dressed as a man but she smiled, because her mistress never ceased to surprise her.

Ema brought a walking stick with her that hid a long stiletto inside, and she tucked Natalie's hand in the crook of her arm and they strolled off into the night. With a hat shadowing her face, her identity could not be discerned, especially since Ema was taller than most women were. The docks were not far off, and she hoped to blend into those who waited until the cock's crow to end their celebration.

Flickering candlelight shone from the front windows of boarding houses and taverns next to the levee. Loud conversations and snatches of music drifted in the air. Sailors, travelers and soldiers were celebrating Mardi Gras to the fullest.

Ema saw pairs of men stationed here and there, and she knew Noel Girod sent them out to search for his sister. Natalie's grip tightened on her arm, which showed she saw them as well. As Ema expected, they did not fit the description of whom they sought, and they continued without being stopped.

Taverns still discharged drunken sailors into the night, where they stumbled off to find a bed. Far off the bobbing lights of anchored ships dotted the darkness, and the sound of lapping waves broke the silence. Under a flaming torch, Ema saw a lanky sailor with a green scarf tied around his neck. The man glanced around, and his eyes widened when he realized that the man turned out to be a woman.

"My friend, take us to the boat." Ema commanded him.

He did not say a word but indicated for them to follow him down a narrow pier. At the end, a long rowboat waited. Natalie cried out in gladness when she saw Captain Holbet's face staring up at them. He climbed up and embraced her. She stifled a sob against his shoulder, and he whispered words of comfort into her ear. He told the sailor to climb down, and then he helped Natalie into the boat.

Captain Holbet turned back to Ema, and he could not hide his surprise upon seeing her outfit. "Madame, I am unfamiliar with how you learned your ways, but I cannot argue that you have saved us. Please thank Mr. Beasley, I hope to meet with him and do it personally when he comes to New York."

Ema lowered her gaze, because how could she explain to him that meeting would never take place.

"I will convey your message to him, but he asked if you would grant him this small favor. Please take this mail to his solicitor when you reach New York. Their name and address is written outside, but do not let anyone know. Captain Coffin is in charge of other papers, but he asked in particular you deliver these and ask them to read their contents in your presence."

Ema handed him a packet of sealed letters, and he responded, "But of course, it will be my pleasure."

Captain Holbet cleared his throat, unsure how to proceed. Ema waited expectantly.

"Madame, I am a Christian man, and now that I will leave here without the ability to help in this matter, my conscience will not allow me to sail away to a happy future."

"Continue sir." Ema encouraged him.

"I came to have knowledge of Noel Girod's plan, when a group of us gathered at a cabaret run by Carlota D'erneville. That same night I overheard a sub-lieutenant from the brig *Lyon* laughing at how his captain came home to find his wife cuckolded him. She gave birth to a child the week before his ship sailed into New Orleans. It is impossible the babe is his, since his voyage lasted over a year."

"He described his captain as being a vengeful man, but he dare not strike out against his wife, whose family protected her and would bring him up on charges of murder regardless of the reason. However, he has sworn that he is searching for the midwife who assisted in the birth. He is afraid she will speak of this, and he will become the laughingstock of New Orleans."

"What are his plans for this woman? It is no fault of hers that his wife played him false." Ema asked.

"He plans to murder her."

"Maybe he spoke in anger."

"I thought the same, and the sub-lieutenant assured me this man is violent even without provocation. He knows he intends to carry out this threat."

"Who is this woman?"

"Her name is Blanche Beaupre."

"I have heard of her, but I have never met her."

"Madame, then I urge you to carry word to someone who will warn her. I apologize for burdening you with this disagreeable request. Perhaps you can ask Mr. Beasley to handle this affair."

"Not to worry Captain Holbet, I know who to speak to about this. But please leave, the sun will be up soon and none must suspect of where you are."

"Adios Madame, God be with you, and thank you for your help."

He climbed into the boat, and shoved it off the pier, while the sailor took the oars and paddled them away into the darkness.

Ema stood there for a moment, wishing she could be present when Captain Holbet learned from Henry's solicitors that he now owned the *Syren*.

She meandered off the pier and stood still when the smell of rotting meat met her nostrils. It overcame the usual ones of the wharf. She knew it had been absent only minutes ago, but this was not the first time she had smelled it. The nighttime became even quieter, as drinking overcame even the most boisterous. Ema walked slowly as if she were slightly drunk. Soon she knew more than one person followed her.

Juan Campos and John M'Faile were often mistaken for brothers. They both bore evidence of having survived smallpox, but besides their pockmarked face, in actuality they were quite different. Campos was a seaman and M'Faile a purser's steward aboard the *Viper*, a ship they deserted a few days before, with little thought of what awaited them once they did.

Three weeks passed and their money dwindled to nothing. They offered twenty dollars in reward for M'Faile and ten for Campos. They could not stay in the city long before someone turned them over to claim the bounty. They were hungry and desperate, and the lone figure of a man dressed in black seemed an answer to their prayer.

Crime ran rampant in the city, and the newly formed police department could do little to control it. Their hands were full, especially on a day like this. The two men guessed they could carry out their plans without any interference.

M'Faile instructed Campos to circle to the front. He planned to grab the man from behind, and then Campos who stood only five feet tall could approach from the front, and stab him. They hoped the robbery would fill their pockets with badly needed funds.

Ema heard their steps and guessed what their plans were. She noticed something else. Whatever else skulked in the darkness the pungent stink originated with it.

She stopped and brought out a handkerchief and pretended to blow her nose. The one behind her crept closer. Then they heard what sounded like a large bird taking flight, and then a man cried out in terror.

Large wings suspended a nightmare figure in the air. Long, knotted hair blew in the wind across pendulous breasts. A woman with wings for arms, and bird talons instead of feet uttered a blood-curdling shriek. She swept down and clawed at the man's face, gouging his eyes out. He screamed in pain and flailed his arms about trying to free himself.

The man behind her called out, "Juan, Juan, what is it?"

Forgetting about Ema, he ran up to help his friend, only to fall back when he saw what lifted him by the shoulders and carried him away. Juan's face dripped with blood, and in its place were shreds of hanging skin.

The creature's contorted features hung in the air, and the stink coming from her made him gag. She screeched at him with an unearthly call. The harpy tried to leave, but the man's limp form started to struggle again and she came back to the ground with it. She covered his thrashing body with her own and started to bite at his face, swallowing chunks of meat. He stopped moving.

M'Faile stumbled backwards, fell down, picked himself up and ran off in the levee's direction. The man he intended to rob did not exist, eclipsed by the terror grabbing his heart.

The harpy stared at the dark figure that scrutinized her in silence. It cocked its head to one side, gore dripping from her chin.

DIABOLIQUE
A Sibyl Novella

Ema took her hat off and came closer to her. Her hair became undone and flowed in a strong, cool rush of wind that came out of nowhere.

"Surprised to see me Thuella? You have aided my enemies and thus made yourself one of them. There is none to stay my hand, including you." Ema spoke in a language not heard for thousands of years.

The harpy stared at the red-haired woman, understanding only too well what she meant.

"Powerful Sibyl, ignorance is my only defense. I did not know you pursued the Scrutator demon. They promised me delicious food to devour, as much as I wanted, and I could not deny the hunger that plagues my being. Here in this place of men…"

"Where you do not belong." Ema finished her sentence. "Why waste more time? Do I expect any less than my enemy should lie to me?"

The thing answered in a raspy, gurgly voice. "Do not call me your enemy."

"Then tell me who brought you here. Do not lie any further and tell me the Scrutator demons summoned you, because we both know they do not have the ability or the knowledge to bring you forth."

An intense silence surrounded them. Suddenly the sound of deep breathing came from the swamp. The harpy's pale features showed terror. Ema could see she feared whatever watched them from the inky black surrounding them.

Ema said in a thoughtful voice, "So now you are the hunted. How many times have you escaped from it before tonight?"

Thuella the harpy glanced back at Ema, and then once more stared with eyes full of fear into the shadowed swamp.

"Now you realize other creatures are here that will devour you the same way you did this man."

They heard cracking branches, and they knew it waited only for the harpy. Ema considered offering Thuella safe passage back to the dimension she belonged in, when unexpectedly she screamed shrilly and launched itself into the air. She flapped her wide wings, and she barely cleared the trees when Ema heard the creature crashing through the swamp in pursuit of her. Then something large launched itself from the trees and grabbed the harpy by one of its clawed legs, pulling it into the trees.

Ema could hear the harpy scream in pain, then she heard the crunching of bones, and the odor of blood filled the air. Other noises nearby alerted Ema that more than one creature joined in gorging on the harpy. The red-haired woman, scooped her hair up, and set the hat back on her head. She knew she held no allure to what hunted in the swamp. She resumed walking back towards Bourgoine Street.

The sun lightened the eastern horizon when she lay next to Henry's body and dissolved into him. Before she drifted off to sleep, she realized there was dark sorcery afoot, and she was the target.

11. A Dish Best Served Cold

The next morning Ash Wednesday dawned clear and cold. Henry Beasley took Isabel, and a freshly scrubbed Pepin in the phaeton. Isabel had questioned the boy, and he told her his name was Jose Andres Belasko. His father died on the voyage from Spain, and his mother scraped by selling flowers. Two years before the fever claimed her and his younger brother.

The square in front of the church was deserted, and inside their steps echoed in its emptiness. Père Antoine waited for them in front of the baptismal font where he performed the sacrament.

Afterwards, Henry pulled Père Antoine aside, and negotiated with him a series of donations; to be paid during the time, Pepin attended classes. He asked the priest to find two other boys who were poor and illiterate so they could be schooled together in private by one monk. The pastor agreed, and like many who surrounded Henry Beasley, attributed his change of demeanor to his brush with death.

At the end of the conversation, Mr. Beasley asked about Blanche Beaupre. He learned that she left to spend a few days with relatives in Mobile. Henry told Père Antoine he wished to thank her for sending Isabel and that he planned to hire other servants based on her recommendation, but he could wait for her return.

The short, balding man put his expensive hat on, and told the priest he could speak in total confidence to Madame Duplessis about all matters. Then Père Antoine inhaled sharply because he could have sworn Mr. Beasley's eyes were a deep green, instead of the gray they usually were. Henry turned around and made his way towards where Pepin and Isabel waited for him.

Soon afterwards, the people of New Orleans drifted in to begin the Lenten season, and to be marked with repentance ashes on their forehead. The cathedral filled up, and then Noel Girod entered accompanied by an older woman with up swept white hair and stern features. He pushed a man seated in a three-wheeled invalid chair.

Noel's haughty gaze swept the crowd and stopped when they met Henry's gray eyes that did not blink or dart away. He'd not seen the man since the day he sighted through his pistol and shot him, he thought, through the heart. He appeared different, younger, and this thought irritated him.

The mass concluded, and the people left, most to recover from the prior day's carousing. A cloudless sky greeted them outside, and a cool breeze swept through the groups who traded gossip *sotto voce* about scandalous behavior from the previous night. Natalie Girod's name circulated among all of them. There were comments and knowing glances, about a tall man seen conversing with Natalie before she disappeared. He stood out since he didn't wear a costume in a masquerade ball full of people dressed in gaudy and outlandish outfits. Many recognized him as the sea captain that romanced Mademoiselle Girod months ago.

Noel Girod stood speaking to his mother Assiline.

DIABOLIQUE
A Sibyl Novella

"They are all laughing at us," she whispered to him, "if this Captain Holbet is the one who took her, we must find where they are. Her reputation is ruined, but if they find a priest to wed them, then we will have no say so in this matter."

Noel knew only one person who had this information. His eyes sought Henry Beasley in the crowd, and it gave him satisfaction to have a reason to confront and humiliate the merchant in front of those who stared at him with mocking eyes.

Heads turned to stare at him as he approached Henry who stood speaking to another merchant. Isabel's friends surrounded her and Pepin, as they conversed not far off from Mr. Beasley's watchful eye. The cook stared at the tall man with saturnine features who addressed Henry in a cold tone.

"Beasley, I must speak to you regarding one of your employees."

Henry excused himself from the conversation and stepped away to speak to Noel Girod.

His gaze and voice were steady. "Which employee do you speak of Girod?"

"Holbet, he is the captain of one of your ships."

"What would you like to know?"

"Where is he?"

Henry shrugged his shoulders. His manner remained calm and unaffected, something that angered Noel. "Girod, I do not know where he is. What I care about is that he shows up to sail the ship to her next port. I think he is on the ship, or at a boarding house near the levee."

"I want to search the ship."

"You do, why?"

Noel Girod's swarthy face colored as he answered between gritted teeth. "My sister Natalie has disappeared. I think he kidnapped her."

"Kidnapped? Then you should speak to the police. I do not involve myself in the personal affairs of others." Henry smiled as he continued, "Have you considered she left with him without being coerced, and now she is Mrs. Holbet, the wife of a sea captain?"

Noel's hand balled into a fist. "My sister disgrace her family in this manner; never! I will find her and that dog Holbet. I will start by searching the ship."

Henry's pale eyes stared at the tall man. "Girod you may do whatever you wish concerning your sister, except for one thing. You will not search the ship. If I find you or someone you employ aboard her, it will have dire consequences for the intruder. As you know, the law sides with a property owner defending their own."

Nicholas Girod raged inside, but stood staring at a man who only a few weeks ago he goaded into a duel. Beasley summoning the authorities was assured if anyone went to search the boat. He could not afford a scandal of that nature. He had friends in high places, but so did the merchant.

Henry then smiled again. "I wanted to mention a strange coincidence. Recently I purchased a small cottage on Burgoine Street, I believe your childhood nurse Bosette lived there until she died. I did not know of this until afterwards. Imagine, it stood empty for several years and I got it for practically nothing. It had developed a reputation for being haunted. How quaint."

Noel Girod blanched. Henry Beasley could see his thoughts playing out on his face. He wondered if the man he tried to kill knew the truth of the horrible crime he committed in the house.

Henry turned to see Madame Girod pushing the man in the invalid's chair to where they stood. Her mouth was turned down at the corners, and her demeanor exuded outraged pride.

She swept up to Henry, and her voice trembled with indignation, "Monsieur, my son has told me you have knowledge of where my daughter Natalie is. It is your duty as a gentleman to help locate her at once."

Henry bowed his head, and said in a dispassionate voice, "Madame, they have misinformed you; I do not know where Natalie is."

"But of course you will deny this, you are protecting your employee. I should expect no less from the likes of you."

"Madame, I do not know what you expect, and to be frank I do not care. I am doing what a gentleman does to safeguard their reputation, which is to avoid involvement in a tawdry affair. There is something *dangereuse* about your family." Henry tapped his chest where a wound still healed from Girod's bullet.

The woman's mouth sagged open in disbelief. She was not accustomed to being spoken to in this manner. She turned to her son which she believed by now would have stepped into correct this impudent man. Nicholas' eyes blazed with fury, but he stood silent.

Henry saw him grab the older woman by the elbow to pull her back before he turned to the man who sat in the three-wheeled chair made of rattan. He noticed that for being an invalid he appeared to be in remarkably good health. He had an ageless quality to his appearance. His cheeks were red, his lips full and a deep pink color. Dark brows arched over twinkling black eyes. A full beard circled his face, and wavy black locks fell to his shoulders. A blanket covered his legs, but his chest and shoulders were broad.

The man grinned. "Monsieur, let me introduce myself. My name is Julian Saturno. Please understand that Madame Girod is overcome with worry, and we must forgive mothers when they are desperate to find a beloved child."

"I am not heartless Monsieur, but it is wrong of me to give her false hope."

"But you will come to us right away if you become aware of any tidbit of information that will help us find our Natalie."

"You may depend upon it." Henry extended his hand and bowed closer to smile into the man's face. When he clasped Julian's hand, Ema's green eyes glinted back at him. He let go of Henry's hand as if it burned with the hottest fire. The mirthful smile fled from his face.

"Nicholas, your mother is tired, let us return to Marysas." He turned back to Henry, "A pleasure Monsieur Beasley".

DIABOLIQUE
A Sibyl Novella

Nicholas Girod pushed the man along, and his mother came behind him. The three of them were grim-faced. Curious eyes followed them, because none of those standing in front of the cathedral dared leave. It entranced them watching the interaction among the players. They promised to be the subject of every conversation that evening and for days to come.

Once they were under way, Henry turned to Isabel. "Do you know the name of the man accompanying the Girod family?"

"Señor Saturno is the overseer of their plantation Marysas."

"An overseer confined to an invalid's chair?"

"He has several men following his every order, and even Madame Girod and her son obey his instructions. He is the one that has made the family rich. Nicholas Girod does not like this to be commented upon for obvious reasons."

"I find it hard to believe that Madame Girod bows her head to anyone."

"He worked at her family's plantation in Mobile before she married. When her husband died, he came to them, but even then he could not walk."

Henry Beasley stopped for a moment, then continued in a thoughtful tone, "How odd, he appears hardly older than Noel Girod."

"This is not the only thing that is unusual, but I shall not gossip about this subject."

Henry turned to Isabel who lowered her eyes. "Come Isabel, tell me the stories you've heard. I know the marketplace has truths that are never uttered in the drawing rooms for fear of offending the ladies."

"Very well Señor Beasley, many people have commented on how alike Monsieur Girod and Monsieur Saturno look. This is another reason they say M'sieur Noel does not like the overseer to go to the city."

"Well, well, that puts a different light on the subject."

The rest of the ride to the house on Burgoine Street continued in silence.

12. Blood Sacrifice

Two days later Nicholas Semple met with Henry Beasley. The *Venus* left as planned, but they faced a serious problem, William Holbet was missing. Semple stood with crossed arms, staring at Henry who appeared unaffected by this potential loss of revenue.

"Henry, the ship has been loaded, and they are waiting for her in Charleston. She will arrive full of merchandise from end to end, and the goods have been sold to merchants in that city. I don't know how you guessed the future scarcity of these items, but we are the only ones in possession of them. Once the hold is empty, then the cargo in Charleston will be brought onboard, but without a captain, New York might as well be the moon."

"New York is not that far away Semple."

Nicholas studied Henry Beasley and then an obvious thought came to him. "You know where Holbet is. We have seen neither him nor Mademoiselle Natalie since the Mardi Gras ball. By God, they are together and you know where they are."

Henry kept his composure and did not betray any emotion. "Nicholas I do not know what you're talking about, but you are right, we must find a captain. Isn't your brother-in-law a first mate on a schooner? You mentioned he arrived in New Orleans two weeks ago."

"I did not think of him."

"Would you trust him to take the ship to New York?"

"Yes, he has sailed to different ports, including the Far East."

"Then the problem is solved. Ask him if will take the job as captain, and if he can sail in three days."

Nicholas Semple straightened up and his face brightened. "I am positive he will agree."

"Upon his assent, start provisioning the ship."

Nicholas' face became solemn, and his voice lowered. "Henry, at some point you will be suspected in aiding Holbet elope with Natalie Girod. Her family might come to you seeking redress."

"Suspicion is not evidence, and I believe many will be happy for the couple. I heard his intentions are honorable, and I will address the situation if it arises."

"Short of shooting him, I believe you have gotten your revenge on Nicholas Girod."

In a change of subject, Henry with curiosity shining in his eyes, said, "What can you tell me regarding the overseer at the Girod plantation? His name is Julian Saturno."

"Ah Henry, I see you are not ready to let this Girod affair end with Natalie's elopement. Very well, he is a mystery. Seldom does he come to New Orleans, but despite being crippled, he has made their plantation very productive."

"What else do they say about him?"

"Sometimes I forget you have been in the city only a few years. Soon after Nicholas' father died, he arrived. He served Madame Girod's family on their farm in Mobile. It did not take long for tongues to wag that Nicholas and Julian resembled one another. This story is substantiated by another story, unproven but not difficult to believe."

"Which is?"

"It is surprising to think a man with no use of his legs is so attractive to the ladies, but such is the case with Monsieur Saturno. He dallied with the governess to the Girod girls. When her belly grew round with child, it came to Madame Girod's attention. The woman threatened to kill the poor governess, and none doubted she could since she acted like a mad woman. Saturno wisely spirited the girl away."

"Unquestionably the actions of a jealous woman."

"Yes, this gossip circulated in hushed tones. Most Creole women avoid a subject that offends decorum, but in truth, most ladies do not involve themselves with whom their overseers bring to their bed. A demand for a marriage or an inconspicuous dismissal is the favored outcome of a disagreeable situation of this type."

"Apparently he made amends and achieved forgiveness. All's well that ends well."

Nicholas chuckled, "Not that quickly, Henry, there is more to this story."

"So Madame Girod holds a grudge; I am not surprised. Satisfy my curiosity and tell me what occurred?"

"Saturno did not marry her, but he did set her up in a small house. He even conceived a second child with her. Then one day they found her murdered in the swamp. From what I understand, they could barely recognize the mangled body. Many asked themselves what animal leaves a carcass uneaten. Saturno sent the children to Cuba to be raised by their grandparents. He paid for their keep and education, and their future is assured, but the murder of their mother remains unsolved. He never set up house with another woman again."

"Could this murderer still be at large?"

"What!" Nicholas said in alarm.

"Read this from today's newspaper." Henry slid the paper towards Nicholas. He grabbed it and started to read:

The Mute Witness to a Terrible Crime - A Murdered Woman's Body Found Floating

New Orleans, February 9. (Special)

This morning a trapper found in an accumulation of drifts in the river the body of a white woman floating face downward and badly mutilated. He secured it to the bank and then notified the coroner who hastily summoned a jury and visited the place where the body was found.

A careful examination was made of it but no wounds were discernible except on the head, the skull being fractured. Nearly all the hair, which was dark, was gone, and one arm and the face had been cut off. The remaining hand and the feet were very small. The body was entirely nude, except that a stocking was on one foot and the waistband of a dress still remained. Around the right ankle, a rope was wound several times and knotted securely. It is reasonably supposed that a weight to sink the body had been attached to the other end of the rope, and that this had slipped off in some manner.

The remains are thought to be those of a young woman about 4 feet 6 inches in height. They had evidently been in the water some time.

The jury felt no doubt that foul play was indicated by the circumstances and accordingly returned a verdict that the deceased came to her death at the hands of a person or persons unknown.

It is hardly likely that any of the facts will ever be known, but no one who saw the body doubts that somewhere a terrible crime has been committed.

The remains were interred today on the riverbank, near the spot where they were found.

"I believe this poor wretch met her end on Shrove Tuesday." Nicholas surmised.

"Or the first day of Lent; perhaps a coincidence or maybe not."

"Henry, I've never known you to be intrigued by these murders."

"You're right, it's just the conversation about Saturno that brought it to mind."

"Well, I will be on my way to speak to my brother-in-law, and I will confirm with you on his answer."

Henry sat at his desk, and remembered the conversation with Tante Ange, and the warning given by the demon that came to attack Père Antoine. Did the start of Lent signal the beginning of a time for blood sacrifices? Another question begged an answer: who buried the murdered woman in unhallowed ground, on the riverbank where her body lay like a piece of trash? Even paupers received a Christian burial in the corner of a cemetery, especially as no evidence of suicide existed. Someone in authority followed a dark agenda, and the visit to Belle Mer could not be delayed any longer.

13. Belle Mer

The late morning sun filtered in through the window of the shuttered room. Henry's body slept in the bed. Ema dressed again in a man's garb, but there were no fine silks or stitched cuffs, the outfit sewed of sturdy clothing protected a rider cutting through fields and swampland. With practiced fingers, she braided her long hair and coiled it in a neat bundle at the back of her neck.

She turned to the far corner of the room, after sensing a sudden drop in temperature. Celeste's white face stared at her from the darkness, and then she glided out. Again, her mouth did not move, but Ema heard her words in her mind.

Her voice sounded raspy, but it had regained a younger tone, more like what she sounded when alive. "I come with thanks and a warning."

Ema nodded to the shade.

"My sister has escaped and she will have a chance at happiness. The gladness that filled me has lifted me from the dark place I have existed in for so long. Sometimes I hear my father calling me, but I cannot find him. But perhaps I will soon; my thanks for saving my sister."

"And the warning?"

"My brother is consumed with fear and rage now that he knows who lives in this house. Finding my sister is secondary, and he even wonders if she is hiding here. He is planning by stealth to enter this house. He does not face the true motive for his actions."

"What is the truth?"

"He is hoping he will find Henry Beasley asleep and kill him and any other occupants, including my sister and her lover. This murder will assuage his blood lust and free him of the fear his crime will be discovered. Your servants are in great danger."

"I thank you for your message, and I hope you and your father find each other."

The ghostly face, smiled faintly, but overall it remained the face of a corpse. She stepped back into the corner and dissolved.

Once downstairs Ema called Isabel and Pepin to the dining room of the small cottage.

Pepin rushed in with flushed cheeks, "Madame the horse is ready as you asked with Señor Beasley's saddle."

"Very good Pepin, but now I must speak to you of a serious matter."

Isabel wiped her hands on her apron and pulled the boy to her.

"We are listening Madame."

"Do you trust me?"

Both of them nodded their head.

"I ride to Belle Mer, but I must leave someone to guard you while I am gone."

"Who, Señor Beasley?"

"No, he cannot defend you against what you saw me battle on the road." Isabel nodded with rounded eyes as Ema continued, "I must leave someone here who will appear unusual, but I do not want you to fear him. He will not harm you. He is here only to protect you."

"Like the large, black dog?" Pepin queried.

"Yes, but different. You will see him only once, and then he will disappear, but he will be vigilant and neither a man of flesh and blood nor a spirit can enter here, but you must not leave the house or the field. Do not open the front door, even if the messenger pretends they come on my behalf or claim someone has hurt me. It is only a ruse."

Isabel and Pepin, both with wide eyes nodded their head again.

Ema then blew on the palm of her right hand, and a blue cube appeared and started to rotate. The glow colored her face in shades of blue, and then it started to grow, and then expanded to a figure that stood over seven feet tall. The shoulders widened, and then it took the form of a male figure with a jackal's head. It held a spear in one hand and filled the room with its presence. The figure bowed to Ema.

"Guard them." were her only words.

The figure nodded and dissolved into dancing blue lights that rose in the air and disappeared.

Ema studied her servants who stood with an overwhelmed expression on their faces.

"I wish I could explain this situation fully, but I promise you there is no Evil in any of my actions."

"That is enough for me Madame, I will make sure Pepin stays with me."

Eleven miles from the outskirts of New Orleans, Belle Mer's main house sat in the distance, off a cypress-shaded road. Built on the same side of the river, it extended all the way to Lake Pontchartrain. Of its two hundred acres, three quarters of it rustled with Creole cane. There were still acres left uncultivated from which extended a swamp of virgin cypress. One field grew corn for human and animal consumption. A white picket fence surrounded neat squares of the vegetable garden. A kitchen, blacksmith forge, slave quarters and a sugarhouse surrounded a raised cottage. Steps led up to a wide verandah that ran the length of the house. The ground floor, cooler in the summer, was used to store foods and other supplies.

No smoke came from the main house or the blacksmith's forge. No humans milled around engaged in their daily chores. None noticed the figure astride a horse watching from under the shade of a large cypress tree. Then a loud crying filled the silence of the afternoon. A wail of despair that Ema knew only heartbreak from an unexpected death could produce. Two horses stood tethered at the front of the house.

A man came out to the wide verandah on the second floor and stood staring to where Ema sat astride Alegria. He saw her and came down the stairs, mopping the back of his neck and then his brow with a red scarf. He settled a large-brimmed hat on his head, mounted a horse and galloped out to where she waited.

The man's face remained grim, and he halted the horse a few paces away.

"Who are you and what do you want?" he asked in an unfriendly voice.

Ema removed her hat and lowered the scarf around the lower part of her face. "My name is Madame Duplessis, and yours?"

The man's eyes widened with surprise when he realized a woman sat astride the horse.

"Madame my apologies, I did not expect you. My name is Francisco Azure, I am the steward."

"No need to apologize. I stopped here because it sounds as if there is trouble at the house. What has occurred?"

Ema could see the man weighed what he should say to her. "Ah Dios mio, I do not know where to begin."

"Do not worry. Tell me the truth as best you know it, even if you don't understand it."

The man with his sunburned face studied her with searching eyes. Her steady gaze for some strange reason comforted him. Her firm voice carried an undertone of kindness.

He thought, "What is the worst that could happen? He could lose his position; but perhaps this was for the best. He would tell her the truth."

He commenced his story, "Late in the night a man came running out from the sugarcane fields. He screamed in terror and asked for our help. He told us he is an Acadian, and he accompanied his cousin on a hunting trip into the swamp. Something attacked them. You could see claw marks upon him, and he repeated the word 'loup garou'. The slaves became panicked. For several days, they heard the howl of a wolf which started when the sun was setting, but no wolves roam this land, unless it those that are men by day, and transform at night to hunt other humans."

Ema remained silent, listening intently to his every word.

"The overseer took a slave with him and went into the swamp to search for the other hunter and to find the animal responsible. He knew the slaves feared going to work the next day, already they were hesitant and now with proof that something roamed afield killing humans, no threat could induce them to leave their quarters. I warned him not to go, to wait until dawn, but he did not listen."

"What did he find?" Ema asked, expecting the answer beforehand.

"The slave Martin, who accompanied him ran back not even an hour later. Blood and gore covered him from head to toe. He said that something pounced on the overseer, but not a real animal, because it walked like a man. The thing carried away the overseer's body. At first light, I went in search of the man, even though I held little hope of finding him. I knew Martin did not lie, the fear in his eyes spoke the truth."

Francisco Azure rubbed his eyes, as if trying to remove what he saw from his memory.

"You found the overseer?"

"What little remained of him. His body lay disemboweled between the roots of a cypress tree. Whatever took him fed on his innards; the extremities were left uneaten. We brought his body back, and tried to keep his wife from seeing him, but she broke away and saw what no woman should have to see. We never found the other hunter, but I will not lie to you, I did not search for him after finding the overseer."

"Madness has descended upon this land Madame. I have a half-crazed woman, a wounded man who only whispers prayers, and slaves who refuse to leave their barracks. The devil is loose, but do not be tempted to think we are madmen, for I swear upon my soul what I have told you is the truth."

"Then I chose a good day to come here."

"Perhaps, but I cannot assure your safety. I urge you to return to New Orleans, but I know the road is not safe at night."

"I will stay in the house."

"Madame, give me time to have things readied for you. The house is unoccupied."

"Unoccupied?" Ema asked with a raised brow.

"Neither the overseer nor I live there. We have our own houses behind this one. There is something disquieting filling this place. Those sent to clean it, will only do so during the daytime."

"What is wrong?"

"There is coldness there. Something unseen drifts from room to room bringing a chill with it. After Don Ambrosio came to live here, something changed, and I have been tempted to ask a priest to come and bless it."

"We shall see." Ema commented. They walked the horses back to the house in silence.

On the first floor of the house, a bloodstained cloth draped over the overseer's body that lay on a table. Mr. Azure's wife who acted as housekeeper held a woman who rocked back and forth. A man with a bandaged eye, and an arm in a sling sat in a chair. In his other hand, he held a rosary, and Ema could see him mouthing the Hail Mary.

"Where are your children?" Ema asked Francisco Azure.

He steered Ema away from the group. His face colored, and he answered in measured tones, picking his words, "Madame Duplessis, even before these events this place has been plagued by something unholy. When I came to work here a decade ago, rumors circulated that a creature stalked the swamps. I came from Cuba to take this post and knew nothing of these stories. It was not long before I learned the truth. A beast stalks men or women if they stray far into the marshes. The grounds of the house, the outbuildings and the slave quarters are a sanctuary where this creature will not venture. In the fields there is no protection."

"Soon after I arrived, I wanted to prove only an animal grown used to eating human flesh prowled through the fields. I went out by myself as the sun set in the west, and before long I became the hunted. My horse bolted, almost throwing me from the saddle. It did not stop until it reached the stables. Without a horse, I would have died that day."

"I have seen things through the years that have convinced me that no human should be in the fields once the day is ending. Two months ago something changed, it ventures much closer now. The overseer and I sent our children to stay with my sister in New Orleans. We were not sure we could keep them safe."

"Did you ever tell Don Ambrosio of these events?"

Francisco Azure studied the red-haired woman. He wanted to make sure that what he said did not offend her if she happened to be a friend of the powerful Figueroa family.

"I tried, but he dismissed my words, but then he said something puzzling. 'No creature will ever dare to take what is mine.' Only a few days later he departed, without warning, back to New Orleans and has never returned. Three years have passed and I will not lie Madame, I am glad he has stayed away."

A lanky, black man strode to where Ema stood speaking with the steward. A machete tied at his waist, undisguised fear etched his face.

"M'sieur Azure, they want you to bring a priest. Even now when the sun is out, none will go into the cane."

Ema interrupted before Azure could answer, "Is this Martin?"

"Yes."

Azure turned to Martin and explained that Madame Duplessis came to replace Don Ambrosio. A flicker of recognition crossed his face, and Ema knew Tante Ange sent word ahead.

Ema stood silent after asking him what he saw, without interruption she listened to his story. He described crashing after the overseer and smelling a horrible odor intermingled with fresh blood. Then a howl, deep and guttural sounded nearby. Something moved through the cane, snapping stalks, and then in the lengthening twilight a "demon" that appeared like a dog, but also a human jumped on the overseer and sunk its teeth into his neck. He ran back to the plantation, afraid his end was near.

The man who sat in a corner praying the rosary sidled up to the group, and when Martin finished talking came forward. His hand trembled as he reached out to Ema.

"Madame, I have hunted these swamps since childhood. Some think it is *Père Malfait*, but I know the loup garou pursues men now. For many years, it has taken others living deep in the woods, trappers, criminals and runaway slaves. This is the first time it comes so close. Ride away Madame, return to the city and do not come here again. You will only find death in this accursed place."

14. Egnatius Aulus

Several hours later, Ema sat on the verandah of the main house. She told the steward to take the overseer's wife and the hunter to stay in his home. She took care of making accommodations for herself inside the house. White sheets were draped over the furniture, and no mirrors or religious icons could be found. Any noise echoed, and she could not deny the oppressive feeling held in the silence of a place where no person had lived for years.

Isabel had prepared a basket of food for her. She nibbled at the food and thought of the story the steward had told her. She understood why the loup garou now came so close to Belle Mer. It sensed on a metaphysical level the claim of ownership the vampire wielded dissolved when it fled. Only Tante Ange's magick held it at bay.

Later in the afternoon, Francisco Azure came to check on her, but she could see the exhaustion on his face. She assured him she planned to stay inside the main house, and tomorrow they could discuss what to do next.

The family of the Acadian hunter came to collect him. They were armed and left after offering their thanks. They were eager to be back behind closed doors by the time the day ended.

Nightfall came, bringing the stars and cooler temperatures with it. Ema could hear distant talk and the smell of food being cooked from where the slaves kept close to their quarters.

Ema left a lamp lit next to a window on the second floor and crept through the gloom to the first floor. A tabby cat kept her company as it rubbed against her ankle. It scampered off after a movement and then returned to her mewing to have its ears rubbed.

She held a clear view of the sugarcane fields. A hastily erected scarecrow, planted in the middle of the vegetable gardens, stood as a lonely sentinel. Dried out cypress branches served as its arms and legs. A discarded tricorn hat sat on a desiccated pumpkin head, and a threadbare coat and cloak completed the outfit. A small bell tied to an extended branch tinkled in a breeze blowing through the open space. Insects chirped in their endless song.

Ema watched as a low fog crept in from the swamp and the fields. The night suddenly became silent, and then she heard a noise above her head on the wooden planks of the verandah. The cat hissed and spat in fear, mewling in a high-pitched tone. Above her the thump came again, which she now discerned sounded like a horse. The sound of hooves could not be mistaken for anything else. The cat ran off into the interior darkness, and Ema stood, following the sound of something walking from window to window.

DIABOLIQUE
A Sibyl Novella

Then a movement at the edge of the field drew her eyes. A cloaked, headless figure astride a horse stood there. The animal chomped at its bit, and she could hear the jingle of the harness. From off in the field the unmistakable howl of a wolf reverberated.

Tante Ange's magick did not fetter whatever clomped above her head, but the watchers in the field could not come any closer.

Then Ema saw two red eyes staring from between the growing stalks of the sugarcane. She blinked and tried to make out the body attached to the eyes. Then she made out a wolf's head, dark gray color mixed with black. It appeared mangy and dirty, its fur clumped with dried blood. Then the animal stood on its hind legs, staring with a wicked grin. Jagged teeth filled its long snout. The ears slanted back and the furry body belonged to a human.

Ema realized the noises had stopped, and the loup garou's attention centered on what stood on the verandah above her. The silence was broken when an explosion of running sounded on the wood above her head. It headed in the direction leading to the other side of the field. Ema ran out through a wide portico door in time to see the figure that vaulted down to the ground and turned the corner of the house. She saw a human head and shoulders, so it was a man despite the noise of hooves.

She ran after it and glimpsed a figure running into the cane field. She halted for a moment when her eyes slid downwards and she saw that below the waist, his legs were those of a ram, and a long swishy tail trailed behind it. The creature stopped and glanced over its shoulder. Julian Saturno's eyes filled with fear stared back at her. He kept running into the field. Ema followed him, and then she heard the wolf howl and the unmistakable noise of a horse and rider approaching from the other side of the field, skirting the edges of the compound.

Julian left a trail of broken stalks behind him, which Ema followed easily. She could see the path headed towards the swamp, a treacherous place in the darkness of night. Then she stopped when she heard a cry that sounded like a man yelling in surprise, and the bleat of a goat. She saw above the cane stalks the black horse with its dark rider rear up on two legs. The rider now held a sword in one hand and swung it towards something below it.

She ran forward, her breath vaporizing before her mouth. She came to a narrow field cleared of stalks used to load up carts. Julian Saturno lay on the ground, holding a hand to a deep cut on his upper arm that bled profusely. The black horse reared and stomped its massive hooves before the prostrate form on the ground.

The satyr with his elongated ears turned to her with a face etched in dread. His muscled thighs and legs, which ended in hooves, were those of a goat. His long hair lay matted and full of chaff against the sweating skin of his shoulders.

Ema raced to the space between the horse and Julian to prevent him from being trampled. The headless rider pulled back on the reins to make the destrier rear, its huge hooves slicing through the air in front of it.

"*Volucris!*" she cried out. Spanish moss hanging on the branches of a nearby cypress tree detached themselves. It separated and made itself into three bird-like creatures that flew on swift wings and swooped around the horse's head distracting it.

Ema placed herself between the horse and Julian, as the animal swung its head from side to side, the Spanish moss birds whisking around its eyes. She grabbed the stallion's bridle and ducked her head as she heard the swish of the sword as it cut across the space where her head was seconds ago.

Ema stepped back and scrutinized the figure as he pulled the horse's reins making it prance back and forth. The head on the pommel came alive, it blinked, and then out of its mouth it screamed, "Help me!"

She realized the head belonged to the last person beheaded by the giant sword the figure wielded.

"So you want a new decoration for your saddle?" Ema asked it.

The black horse reared backwards. She sensed it wanted the satyr's head to be the next one riding on the pommel of the saddle.

"Today I will give you the head you do not want."

She clapped her hand once, and it sounded like a gunshot, a well of purplish light opened under her feet, and her clothing melted from her body. Her nakedness became covered by a close-fitting armor that swirled in different colors of magenta, violet and Prussian blue as she moved. It started at her feet and covered her legs, torso and arms in seconds. The Spanish moss birds flew to her as her hair braided itself, and the filaments infiltrated the red tresses, tying themselves at the end.

She opened her right hand palm up, and said, "Zeruko Neskamea." Her sword made of Toledo steel materialized, the pink diamond in its pommel glinting in the oblique dark of the night.

Ema whispered to herself one word, "*Secor.*"

The head on the saddle horn moaned, calling out to be freed.

She turned to Julian who rose on unsteady legs behind her. He towered over her, his chest rippling with muscles. He held his hand over the deep cut on his arm, bright red blood still trickling between his fingers.

"I think I understand who you are now." His dark eyes stared at her in wonderment.

Ema's eyes slid downward, and she could not disguise her surprise when she saw raised, bruised scabs around his ankles.

"Do not run away, something waits for you."

"I know what waits for me there." Julian said with an enigmatic but sad smile on his face.

The forlorn wail of the severed head filled the air, and the rider pointed its sword at Ema. Puffs of white swirled around the horse's nostrils.

The satyr let out a startled bleat as something crashed through the cane towards them. A tall figure entered the clearing. The scarecrow, the cloak fluttering in the wind turned its head towards Ema. The dried branches were now thick, brown and green as if they were part of a living tree. Leaves sprouted in abundance filling the empty jacket, and the dried head fleshed out to ripeness. Large, black eyes blinked in the face, and the holes carved for the mouth and nose moved in animation. The tricorn hat sat perched on the top of what served as its head.

"Julian, your bodyguard." and she indicated the scarecrow with her sword. Green tendrils shot out from the body of the scarecrow and twined themselves around the satyr pulling him close. Leaves covered the cut.

The headless rider leaped from the saddle. It understood Ema's challenge, and that it could not claim Julian unless it defeated her.

She studied the figure and saw that it wore an amalgamation of different military accessories used throughout history. It collected trophies from his victims besides their heads. She even recognized a heavy torque necklace as something Roman soldiers wore.

It sprang at her and thrust forward with its sword, barely missing the side of her head. He lunged at her again. Ema aimed a swift kick at his chest, which turned out to be a mistake. The rider grabbed her leg and the next thing she knew she sprawled on the earth and he stood over her.

She tried to kick at his legs, but they did not give an inch, and he stooped to grab her. Ema pulled him by the forearm and jerked hard. He fell forward, and with swift agility, she regained her feet.

Just as quickly, he came up, and she struck him hard in the chest several times with an armored fist. This did not slow his impetus. She thought to herself, "Fighting something with no head could prove to be a challenge."

The rider and Ema faced each other across the clearing with starlight illuminating them. She guessed his reach measured more than hers did by a few inches. He whipped his blade back and forth as if reading her thoughts.

They parried and thrust at each other and cold sweat beaded her forehead. She knew this creature beheaded many through the centuries, capturing not only their heads, but their souls as well.

Their swords met and locked several times, and Ema understood she could only overcome her opponent one way. She could not best his strength, but every fighter harbored a weakness. Ema waited until he made a flowing, slicing movement towards her chest, exposing his forearm. With a skill born of much experience, in a quick blur the point of her sword pierced through his arm, cutting tendons and burrowing into the rider's chest.

The dark figure staggered backwards. His fingers still gripped the sword's pommel, but the appendage hung useless. A dark, viscous liquid Ema assumed could only be long dead blood trickled from his arm and onto the blade.

Ema knew she needed to bring it under her control. A demonic being had claimed this Roman soldier hundreds of years ago. When mortal, this man must have been a fiend of the first order. No amount of blood or souls could satiate it.

The figure stood there a moment, feeling the vibration thrumming in the air, as Ema summoned a doorway between dimensions. He turned and ran toward the black horse pawing at the ground. Ema whistled, and the animal danced away from his dark master, snorting and refusing to come within arm's reach. She called to the horse in a soothing voice. It pricked its ears up, looked at the woman and with a start crashed against the figure that once rode it, sending him sprawling to the ground. It trotted over to Ema, nuzzling her shoulder.

The man's head stuck on the pommel blinked and opened its mouth and rotting miasma filled the air. "Do not say another word." Ema commanded it.

The headless man, rider no more, sheathed his sword, turned and charged into the sugarcane fields. Ema vaulted on the warhorse's back, and with her knees urged it forward. With a powerful lunge, it galloped after the fleeing figure, its black cape flying behind it. The horse's hooves thundered in the silence.

She knew the headless man planned to run towards the swamp where she could not follow on horseback. With her braid flying out behind her, in a swift movement she sheathed the sword in a halter on her back, which created itself out of the armor she wore. With her finger, she drew a sigil in the air that opened an oval circle; out of it jumped her whip, which she tapped once against her knee and it grew, stiffened and became a long spear.

Ema saw the fast approaching line of cypress trees, which demarcated where the swamp started. With a fluid movement, she threw the spear that screamed through the air and impaled the running figure through the center of its back. Like a pinned bug, it stood unable to move, the spear trapped it in the ground.

She slipped from the saddle, pulled Zeruko Neskamea from behind her and with the tip drew a large circle. The surrounding stalks flattened instantaneously. She then drew a vertical line in front of her that glowed a deep pink in the blue velvet of the night. It elongated and became a doorway. It opened and a pearlescent whiteness shone outward, with a promise of infinite space and calming landscape beyond it.

Out of the white mistiness a figure strode forward dressed in a conquistador's uniform. He held a head in his hand. Deep creases crisscrossed the face and when the eyes opened, the whites were red, and it hissed displaying large fangs.

Ema looked at the head imprisoned on the saddle, a trophy to be tortured. The eyes were closed, and no expression stirred upon it. Ema pulled it from the horn. She turned and threw it to the figure waiting in the doorway that at the same time launched the head he was holding towards her.

He caught it in midair and set it upon his shoulders. The conquistador's body shimmered and changed, and the head became one with the body. The comb morion helmet he once wore appeared on his head, and the eyes opened. He appeared as he once did, animated and with flushed cheeks. He put his gloved hand upon his sheathed sword and bowed to Ema. He then stepped backward into the pearlescent whiteness and dissolved.

DIABOLIQUE
A Sibyl Novella

The head Ema held spit and gurgled blood. The smell of rotting flesh came from it, and she advanced on the body standing impaled. She thrust the head on the shoulders, and like a magnet to steel, it fused. The body writhed, and all the details it gathered from its victims through hundreds of years disappeared. The only thing that remained was the heavy torque around his neck.

The dark clothing changed to the uniform of a Roman centurion. A silver helmet with a transverse crest made of peacock feathers appeared on the head. Muscles were sculpted into the bronze plate covering his chest and stomach. Underneath he wore a red tunic. A blue cloak bordered in yellow and tied with a fibula at his throat materialized.

Ema noticed other measures of his rank were absent, such as a vine-stick cudgel, and a Hispanicus sword which normally rested in a leather scabbard on his left side. Ema wondered what law he broke. Among Roman soldiers, desertion and mutiny were the worse crimes; if they escaped, they faced banishment from Rome. However, there were other crimes such as theft, giving false evidence, sexual misconduct and repeating the same offense three times, which earned a death by cudgeling.

Ema then turned to the warhorse. She uncinched the saddle, blood pooled on the surface of the leather, and it screamed like a thing alive. She threw it to the ground and pulled the bridle and reins from the horse. The animal's black coat became shiny and the mane and tail appeared brushed. It looked like a living animal. A voice called it from within the light, and the horse pricked up its ears in recognition. Ema slapped it on the flank, and it trotted eagerly towards the doorway. Like the conquistador, it disappeared into the opalescent whiteness.

Ema turned to the centurion who still struggled against her spear. "Egnatius Aulus, you will not have need of this entryway. I have a detour in mind for you."

She waved her hand in front of the shimmering door and it closed. It shrank upon itself and became but a pinpoint that disappeared with a pop.

Ema took her sword from the halter on her back and pointed it outward in a circle where the centurion and she stood in the middle. A red line burned itself on the ground, and scarlet smoke poured upwards from it. Four unlit torches erupted from the ground and once above ground flamed to life.

In a voice that crackled like broken glass, and in a language not heard in centuries, Ema cried out, "Come now one who can serve me, and deliver this man's soul to me intact. Come now, one who can purge the unclean from the clean."

A scratchy, deep voice resounded out of thin air, "Allow me entry Sibylline, I will be your servant."

In the same unearthly voice Ema said, "Your name?"

"Orcus, Punisher of Broken Oaths."

"Enter under my dominion."

The air shimmered with a grayish green light and smoke swirled around a figure that coalesced into a tall being with a tusked feral pig's head. Instead of legs, thick snakes writhed underneath it. Its neck and chest were skeletal and bare, and something snakelike moved underneath the skin of the arms. A long, leather loincloth trailed to the floor, and large bat wings folded against its body. The eyes were yellow, and in one hand, it held a long whip spiked at the end.

Ema sized up the figure. Using her normal voice she said, "Enough of the theatrics, this is not a Greek play."

It threw back its head and bellowed in laughter. The greenish mist shimmered once more, and its place stood a tall, muscular man. A beard and tusks sprouted from his lower jaw. The rest of his teeth were jagged. Pig-like ears protruded from between his long, green hair. His skin glowed with a sick yellow tinge to it. In its large ham-like fist, it still held the wicked looking whip. Thick human legs supported his torso, where different snake tattoos writhed and moved across his skin.

Ema's eyes slid to the whip, and he said in a deep voice, "I will use it to deliver what you have demanded, beautiful Sibyl."

"So be it."

Ema strode over to the impaled figure, which still writhed and spat blood. It called out invectives against her, in a long dead language. She backed up, and then made a short run towards the figure, leaped and caught the spear from behind it, and pulled it free. The centurion fell to his knees, and before it could turn its head, the whip in the Orcus' fist flayed its back. The man screamed out in pain.

"On your knees oath-breaker, you are mine now." Its voice now returned to something gravely, deep and unearthly.

Orcas strode to where the bloody saddle and bridle lay on the ground. He flung it through the air, and as if it was something alive, it wrapped itself around the body of the centurion. The straps of the cinch encircled his torso and tightened themselves. The bridle inserted itself inside his mouth ripping the edges of his cheek on either side of his face.

"Since you seem so fond of riding, let us not break with tradition." The Orcas strode over to where the man hunched on all fours, blood pouring from his mouth.

"But, the measurements are not right," the Orcas observed. The whip struck the man on the back of his thighs, and with a crunch of bones, his arms and legs elongated in length so they matched and his hands and feet scrunched and solidified to a hoof-like appearance.

The Orcas mounted his massive weight on the back of the man, took the reins and pulled back sharply. He flicked it with the whip on its tailbone, another crunch of blood and bones, and a leathery tail erupted from his lower back.

"That's better. I believe you will become my favorite mount… in more ways than one, but we have so much time to explore that experience."

The snap of Ema's whip over his head, wiped the smile from the Orcas' face. "Do you forget who stands before you?" her voice pealed like a bell.

Blood trickled from the Orcas' ears. "Forgive great Sibyl, release me and I will take my leave."

DIABOLIQUE
A Sibyl Novella

Ema blew into the air, and the torches disappeared as well as the scarlet circle. The image of the Orcas and the centurion disappeared as the red smoke dissipated.

Normal noises of the night washed in to fill the void of silence. The chirping of insects, an owl hooting in the distance as it hunted for its food, but Ema sensed the eyes of something else that watched her from the gloom.

When Ema arrived where she left Julian, only the scarecrow stood there with broken branches. "Go back." She ordered, and it crackled off into the fields. By the time she came back to the main house, the stick figure leaned as it did before in the middle of the garden, it limbs withered. A lifeless thing meant only to scare away birds.

Once inside the house, Ema sent her armor and her other accouterments into another dimension. She sank into a chair behind her, feeling nauseous and cold at the same time. She touched her forehead, which felt clammy.

It had been many years since she had summoned another being to take a demon into purgatory, and even then, it had been her choice, not out of necessity as tonight. She knew in that moment, she could not complete the task of sending the headless rider into purgatory unaided. Her bravado had masked how vulnerable she was.

These thoughts evaporated as a sharp spasm pierced her chest, and she doubled over with the pain. In an instant, she understood the source of the throbbing. Henry's symptoms were bleeding over into her body. Her ability to mesh with another human, but stay apart at the same time had weakened her to a dangerous level.

A part of her recognized that berating herself did not help, so she quieted her mind and steadied her breathing. The minutes ticked by, and the feelings ebbed away. She blew out the light, dozed in a chair near the window and waited for daylight to tinge the eastern horizon.

15. Neither Forgiveness Nor Mercy

The morning dawned crisp and clear, and the blue of the sky was uninterrupted by even the smallest cloud. She foresaw that she might lose her clothing and brought a satchel with a new coat, shirt, pants and boots. Once dressed she walked to the steward's house. Madame Azure prepared a steaming cup of café au lait for her. Silence filled the house as the overseer's wife slept in another room after a long and tearful night. Afterwards she met with Francisco Azure, who asked her in a hushed tone if she heard the strange noises that trumpeted from different areas of the fields.

"I might have heard something, but I was so tired that I ignored it."

Her next question surprised the steward. "Has Martin learned the duties of an overseer?"

"Yes he does. He learned them all since he came with the overseer from another plantation when he was fifteen years old."

"Call him here."

Ema took Martin aside, and her questions were direct and with no subterfuge. There was no command, only a need for honest answers when time was short and they could not postpone decisions.

He told her yes he knew the duties of an overseer, and he stood stunned when she asked if wanted to be the new overseer of Belle Mer.

"But I cannot Madame, I am a slave."

"Not anymore."

His eyes widened in disbelief.

"Do you have children?"

"Yes, two boys."

"And their mother?"

"Her name is Carmelitte."

"Martin, you must take a surname so I can make this binding on paper. What will you choose?"

He stood for a moment undecided. "Freshet," he said. "this was the overseer's name. He always made sure food filled my belly and there was a shelter to sleep under every night. When he came here, he made sure M'sieur Betancourt agreed to bring me as well."

She bade both men wait for her and she went back into the house. In a few minutes, she returned and gave each of them a paper.

"Martin, this provides proof that you are now free, as is your wife, your boys and any other children you might have. You will now be known as Martin Freshet. I will pay you half of the overseer's salary. In six months if your work is satisfactory I will increase it by a quarter, and in a year, if all is well, then you will receive the equivalent of his full pay."

DIABOLIQUE
A Sibyl Novella

"Merci, Madame, merci." Martin said with tears welling in his eyes.

"I can do this by the authority granted me by the Spanish king over this property to issue this *carta de libertad*. Francisco you are witness to this act, you each have a copy of what I will file when I return to New Orleans. When I return to the city, I will instruct a priest to come here and bless this property."

Francisco Azure stared at the red-haired woman, and he hated to admit it, but a wave of relief flooded over him. He didn't know what to do without an overseer and a piece of land that appeared to be in the devil's grip.

"Martin, as overseer I want you to have a coffin prepared for your predecessor's remains."

"Oui Madame, I will start it without delay."

"I want it sealed with bands of iron and have the blacksmith fashion an iron cross and fasten it to the lid."

Martin and Francisco glanced at each other furtively, neither willing to ask why she made this request.

"When the priest returns to New Orleans, he will take the overseer's remains and his widow back so they can inter him in St. Louis Cemetery."

Francisco Azure said, "I will speak to her of this. I believe she has an aunt living in New Orleans."

"If either of you leaves your position, all I ask is that you give me enough time to find a replacement. Martin if you decide on this, it will not affect your claim to freedom. You can find me in the yellow cottage on Bourgoine Street, or see Père Antoine and he will get word to me."

Ema mounted Alegria.

Francisco volunteered, "Madame Duplessis, let me go with you."

"Do not worry about me. I will inspect the property on my own. I have studied the maps and know what areas belong to this farm."

Ema urged the horse forward, ending the conversation. It cantered briskly away, eager for a run. She skirted the edges of the property, laying down a trail of specially prepared salt and other barriers. When she reached the edge of the swamp, she sat on the horse and surveyed the green darkness shaded by the large branches of cypress trees. She could sense many unnatural things wandered in the depths of the gloomy interior, far beyond the land that belonged to Belle Mer.

Knowing there was much to be done once she reached the city, Ema rode straight through the day and reached New Orleans by late afternoon. She went to St. Louis Cathedral and found Père Antoine in the gardens.

Ema strode in and the priest put away a book under his arm. He studied her with raised eyebrows when he saw her dressed as a man. Then he remembered what he saw her do and wisely determined that she could dress as she pleased.

"Père Antoine, I have just returned from Belle Mer."

"You appear troubled."

"A bit, but I need your help."

"Madame, explain what you need."

"I need for a priest to go to Belle Mer, if possible tomorrow."

"So soon?"

"Yes, I wish him to bless the house and grounds, and perform any sacraments needed among those who live there."

"What is the reason for this urgency?"

"Something killed the overseer, and I wish the priest to go and bring his body back to the city, as well as accompany his widow."

"Killed? How?"

"An animal attack."

Père Antoine stayed silent. He gazed at Ema, and she stared back at him. He knew he should ask no more regarding the circumstances of the overseer's death.

Ema continued, "I do not want his coffin opened again for any reason. The box is bound and locked in iron. By the time his remains arrive here, he will be overdue for burial, which I suggest, should be completed immediately. I will leave this in your hands so that a mausoleum will be ready and have the bill sent to Mr. Beasley."

"I will attend to it and send Brother Clemente to Belle Mer."

It was Ema's turn to widen her eyes in alarm. "No, not Brother Clemente."

"Why not?"

"His brother's reputation is not the best there, and with the overseer's death, things are too unsettled."

"You are right, I did not think of this."

"Père Antoine, perhaps you are not aware the Brother Clemente is seeking to meet with his brother. He is hoping to clear his brother's name or help him. If he ever tells you he has seen his brother, please let me know of this."

"Yes I can understand the peril that Brother Clemente runs both in body and soul should he meet with his brother."

Ema drew out a small bag that clinked with Spanish *reales*. She handed it to the priest.

"I am asking for a priest to return once every week during the time of Lent to Belle Mer. He should perform Mass, and again bless the house, and all the outbuildings of the property. He should be prepared to administer the sacraments if necessary."

A knowing expression came into Père Antoine's eyes.

"Madame, I believe I understand your purpose in this request."

"The following I will leave to your discretion. I wish an iron cross hung in each floor of the main house. There are several empty niches inside the house. I want statues of the Virgin Mary and St. Michael the Archangel to fill them. There are funds to cover the cost in what I have given you, and to help your efforts to beautify St. Louis."

"Madame, rest assured I will give your instructions my personal attention."

DIABOLIQUE
A Sibyl Novella

He blessed her with the sign of the cross, before she slightly bowed her head and strode out into the main square before the cathedral. She pulled on her gloves and squinted her eyes against the setting sun.

Ema rode through the traffic on the Vieux Carre, dressed in her rustic men's clothing. Her copper-colored braid fell down her back, and many men stared at her with admiring glances.

Once she arrived at the small cottage, her body ached and grit scratched her skin. She bathed in a tin tub she kept in a small room added to the back of the house. It was close to the kitchen where she could heat water. The slanted floor sluiced excess water off to the ground.

Several hours later, Ema sat eating her dinner. Isabel came and sat next to her at the table.

"All was well during my absence?"

"Yes Madame, I have found the seamstress you sought. Her name is Dulce, she is the *parda* daughter of Don Eugenio Faillat. He died last year and freed her mother as well as herself and her three siblings. He left them with a property, but they must make a living and she is skilled with the needle. Dulce will take your measurements and work only on your order until completion."

"Very good. Anything else?"

"After you left, I peered out the window, and then after night fell I thought I saw the figure of a man standing on the other side of the road watching the house."

"Did you recognize the person?"

Isabel paused a moment, before continuing. "I cannot be sure, but I believe it resembled Señor Girod. I saw him only once when dusk was descending and then afterwards it was someone else standing there watching the house."

"Yes, our little cottage appears to be fascinating to certain people, but fear not Isabel, all they can do is watch."

The woman nodded and went off to the kitchen.

Ema finished her meal and ascended the stairs to her room. She disrobed and meshed with Henry's body. The ticking clock at the foot of the stairs was the only sound, and occasionally the sigh of a young woman echoed through the hallway. Her misty shade drifted out to a corner of the field behind the kitchen where her bones were the only thing left of her body. Peace eluded her in death, just as it did in life.

16. All Debts Eventually Come Due

The next day Henry Beasley sent Pepin to deliver Madame Duplessis' letters and instructions about Belle Mer to her solicitors. Afterwards, he met with Nicholas Semple who started provisioning the *Syren* to sail to Charleston. His brother-in-law agreed to captain the ship to New York, and because of Henry's urging all efforts were being made to have the ship set sail at the earliest moment.

Nicholas leaned against the mantelpiece that dominated the large room where each of them situated their desks. A slender man, Semple appeared younger than his actual age. He could eat the richest, fattiest food and he maintained the same waistline he enjoyed twenty-five years ago. He always dressed in dark, conservative suits with a simple cravat and a wide-brimmed hat, as a merchant he was one of the most honest and reliable. This was the reason Henry collaborated with him after arriving in New Orleans.

Nicholas crossed his arms across his chest, and with a worried tone to his voice, commented, "Henry, I will admit that when you urged us to leave men guarding the *Syren* at all times, I thought you were being overly cautious. But now I have received reports that Girod's men are always watching the comings and goings."

Henry sat behind his desk, he steepled his fingers and his gray eyes stared at Nicholas before replying, "When will she be ready to sail?"

"In two days."

"I want you to make it known that she will sail in one week instead, because she is waiting to load Cuban tobacco which just arrived today on the schooner *Incroyable*. I want the guard doubled. Tell your brother-in-law she will sail on the original date scheduled. Have him devise a reason why the crew must be onboard the day before she leaves."

"Henry, why this subterfuge?"

"Nicholas, Girod is capable of setting fire to the ship while she is loaded. He knows his sister is not there, but the loss of the ship would be a tremendous blow to us."

Nicholas studied his partner in silence, then said, "Not too long ago Henry, I believed your suspicions were baseless, or at the very least exaggerated, but now I am sure you understand how perverse this man is beyond what anyone in New Orleans suspects."

"I want men hired to guard the warehouse."

Nicholas raised his eyebrows, but after giving it thought, nodded his head before responding, "You are right. The warehouse is full of merchandise. The loss would cripple us financially, but Henry we cannot keep guards on the ship and the warehouse interminably."

"There will be no need; resolution of this problem is at hand. Will you attend to this?"

"But of course, you may count on my full attention to this matter. With that in mind, I will leave now." He took his hat from a nearby hook and left.

Henry read other letters and missives requiring his attention. John Blanque sent a short note that he was interested in Mrs. Manson and if she could come Tuesday next at ten o'clock in the morning to meet with his wife.

He wrote a short note and sent off a messenger with this information to the house on Magazin Street. Then he pulled out a list of his outstanding debts. Every week he wrote a check to pay one of them in full. He did not want any wild rumors to circulate if he should pay everything at once, and he lined through the last two entries.

Later in the evening when Ema disengaged from Henry's form, she studied the man's body that lay still with his chest barely rising with breath. The truth was inescapable; Henry's body was becoming unsustainable at a rapid pace. She knew she would have to use it the least amount of time possible, but soon his heart would stop working, and blood cease to flow through his veins. Her inability to produce a strong boundary between her avatar and herself presented another set of problems that reminded her to tread with caution.

The following day Henry made his morning appearance at his office. Nicholas Semple arrived soon afterwards. They reviewed a list of dry goods advertised for sale that morning.

Nicholas turned to Henry and said, "I forgot to give you the information you requested. The captain of the *Lyon* is Juan Sangster."

Henry's eyes were alert when he asked, "Nicholas what have you heard of this man?"

Nicholas smiled, and replied, "Henry I believe you are a fortune teller."

"Indeed."

"The rumor is that he is selling the vessel. Is this why you have been making inquiries?"

Henry shrugged his shoulders, "Perhaps, continue."

"Sangster and his brother-in-law, Thomas Choate own the ship. I suspect a family scandal is being kept concealed. It concerns a child Captain Sangster's wife gave birth to only a few weeks before his arrival in New Orleans. People who can count on both hands understand she conceived this child when the captain was on the high seas. But, the problem though is that Sangster has made serious threats to kill his much younger wife."

"I heard something along these lines previously, I just did not know it was Sangster who had been cuckolded."

"Young Mrs. Sangster has four older brothers, that though disapproving of her misconduct, point out he spent little time with his wife. He preferred to either be drinking at taverns, sailing to distant ports or in the company of his shipmates. They tolerated this behavior, but not threats made against their sister or her child. They spirited her away to the family's home in Biloxi and insisted that Sangster stay in New Orleans."

"I see, the Choate family has in fact separated them to keep her and the child safe."

"Yes, and they must see no chance at reunification, since Thomas Choate is insisting on the sale of the vessel. I think they also grew tired of having to replace the ship's crew due to Sangster's abominable temper."

"An unenviable position, no wife, no child and now no ship. I am sure it does not improve his reputation over this matter."

"Sangster shall we say, is long in the tooth. He remained unmarried most of his life and only took a wife three years ago. He secured young Miss Choate as a bride because she was a very plain girl, but it appears not plain enough. Now he is an old man, without a ship to captain, which might leave him penniless unless he has been scrupulous with his money. As to his reputation, they know him as a prideful man, no doubt he is a bitter man as well now."

Henry teased Nicholas Semple, "Is that comment meant for me as well?"

"No Henry. True, you have remained unmarried, even though you enjoy female company too much, but you have something to show for it. You have become prosperous and were you not seeking a bride before your duel with Girod?"

"Yes, and I am guilty like Sangster not to recognize how quickly years can slip away between your fingers. You find your contemporaries are now grandfathers, and you wake up to an empty bed and a silent house."

"Then I hope you will continue to seek a woman to wed."

Henry's gray eyes remained serious when he replied, "We shall see Semple, we shall see." He could not tell his friend that only a funeral awaited him.

It was after midnight, and the *Syren* was set to sail on the morning tide. Ema slipped out of the house again dressed in dark, men's clothing. The air was chilly, and she pulled the crown of her hat lower, and tied a scarf around the lower part of her face. She suspected that despite their best efforts to keep the secret of when the ship sailed, Girod knew the truth.

When she approached the levee, she turned down a side street, lined with several boarding houses that catered to those disembarking from a ship. She found a dark niche between two buildings where she could stand concealed and still have a clear view of where the ship lay anchored off in the distance.

Conversation and laughter drifted over from nearby taverns along with the pungent smell of the wharf. Ema could not still the intuitive voice urging her to be here tonight. She leaned against the wall with a patient sigh. She learned through years of experience that it would eventually become clear why she was here.

As Ema ruminated on these thoughts, one floor above her Blanche Beaupre was attending to a pregnant woman who arrived earlier in the day on a schooner. She was late into her pregnancy, but she endured a rough voyage where she could not stop vomiting. This was her first child, and her husband summoned a midwife to be on hand, but once she slept in a bed that did not sway with the waves, and drank broth, her stomach settled. The contractions became further apart and stopped.

Blanche was collecting her things when a soft tap sounded at the door. The husband opened it, and a voice whispered that a message arrived for the midwife. The man paid Blanche, and she stepped outside to the landing.

Juanita, the owner's daughter stood there holding a candle. In its dancing light, she explained someone else needed her services only two doors away. Like this couple, they had disembarked only a few hours ago.

Blanche found there was always a spate of births brought on by traveling on a ship. Juanita guided her to a side door and gave her a small lantern so she could light her way. Blanche pulled her shawl tighter around her, and took a basket with her belongings in one hand, and the lantern in the other.

She stepped out to the narrow street that lay in darkness, lit only by an occasional candle at a front window. While visiting relatives in Mobile, she attended only two births. Now she needed to make money. The woman scanned the darkness but did not see any drunken sailors or soldiers, which usually made their presence known, but she could not shake the feeling she was being watched.

Blanche walked slowly in the darkness, the lamp casting only a small circle of illumination before her. Then a silhouette detached itself from the gloom in front of her, and someone knocked the lantern from her hand. She detected a quick movement and then a piercing pain spread under ribs. Liquid warmth flowed down her belly.

From behind her a deep voice said, "Estupido, cut her throat. Never mind, I'll do it." A hand grabbed her hair and then jerked her head back. The other shadow still stood before her.

She knew the wetness tracing a rivulet down her thigh, could only be her blood. Her consciousness plunged into the redness away from the pain she experienced. Perhaps if she ran away on this stream, she could escape the fear and pain awaiting her when her throat met the blade of a knife.

Her vision became blurred, and she thought of her son, and the many years since she looked upon his countenance and kissed his forehead. She thought of her dead husband, which she knew awaited her in heaven. From far away she heard a scuffle, and the grip on her hair loosened. Her body crumpled, then the downward motion slowed.

Blanche lost consciousness for a moment, but then when she opened her eyes, she was standing up. She wrapped a bandage around her midsection and then tied her shawl around it to cinch it in close to her body. It was the queerest sensation because she could not control her movements; only watch her fingers nimbly tie a knot. She opened a blanket she carried with her, dropped several items of clothing into it and stuffed it into her basket. She stepped over two figures lying on the ground, and then she swirled into a deep well of forgetfulness.

The midwife drifted through the streets, keeping to the murky depths. Only once, did an inebriated sailor come up to her, only to hear a gravelly voice warn him away. He stumbled backwards and ran into a darkened side street.

She let herself into a house on Bourgoine Street and went to a small bedroom in the back. She let her bloodied gown fall at her feet and then took a clean sheet to tie around her waist. The flow of blood had been staunched from a wound inflicted on the side of her abdomen caused by the point of a knife. After pulling back the covers, her form became limp, and Ema's naked figure shimmered and materialized next to her. Ema stood and scrutinized the form of her new avatar. Now she understood the inevitable pull that drew her to stand in the cover of the boarding house.

Since the time she joined with Blanche's body, she gathered information about her. Memories, even the forgotten ones, sensations both good and bad flooded Ema's being. She was a middle aged woman, a bit overweight, but overall in good health. Death for her would have been inevitable if her attacker had sliced her throat. The stab wound in her side was not deep and did not hit any organs. Ema conversed with Blanche's spirit, and they understood each other, but on a conscious level, she needed to accept what it meant to be Ema's pocket.

This was a crucial point, for if Ema sensed an incompatibility with the person as a sentient avatar, she released them into a quick and peaceful death. There were many human qualities she detested, such as greed, laziness, cowardice and the inability to feel compassion. Henry and avatars like him demanded no vetting, accepting a pocket with their own personality required caution.

Ema changed into a simple gown and sat next to Blanche for the next few hours until dawn broke. The woman slept deeply, and her forehead felt cool to the touch. She walked out to the kitchen where Isabel stoked the fire inside the oven.

She explained to Isabel what happened and why she brought Blanche back to the cottage after being attacked. Ema warned her not to speak of the midwife's whereabouts in order to protect her.

By the time, Isabel returned from the market, Henry sat at the dining room table sipping tea and Ema was gone. Isabel served him breakfast, and she watched him, noticing how he appeared to be wasting away. His waistcoat which used to bulge with a belly, hung loose. His thin face belied a person not long for this world.

Later in the morning, Henry sat at his desk going through bills of lading when he heard Semple's footsteps on the stairs leading to the door. Nicholas opened the door and hung up his hat and a scarf.

"Henry, have you heard the news regarding the murders?"

"No Nicholas, I have not. Is it another woman dumped in the river?"

"No, it was two men."

"But I can tell by your demeanor there is something unusual about their deaths."

"Yes, not because someone murdered them; they are thugs commonly hired for nefarious purposes. It is the manner of their death causing a stir."

Henry leaned back in his chair, and with an impassive face gave Nicholas his full attention.

"I take it was grisly?"

"Yes, both of them had their throats slashed from ear to ear, but the cuts were cauterized as if the killer used a burning, hot knife. The word is the devil came to claim his own."

"Perhaps, he did."

Ema thought, "Nicholas I wonder what you would think if you knew you stood before the person who committed that act?"

"Whether it was the devil or not, this Sunday the sinners of New Orleans will fill St. Louis to the rafters. There are many that fear Satan is collecting souls during Lent."

"Well then, some good will come of the murders after all."

"Henry, always the pragmatist, but let us speak of pleasant topics. The *Syren* has set sail with her cargo intact."

"Then we are successful, but I suspect Girod will not accept I have bested him."

A message arrived interrupting their conversation, and then plans were made about a sale to take place later in the day at the Coffee Exchange House. Nicholas left to attend it.

Henry sat quietly behind his desk. Inside of him Ema thoughts turned to Julian Saturno and visiting Marysas Plantation to speak directly to him. There were many questions she needed answers to. Was Julian protecting Nicholas Girod, and if so, why? How many others had Noel Girod murdered? She could sense the swirl of dark magic surrounding him. Nicholas' confrontation, which ended in duels, was a clever ruse to disguise a bloodlust. This was a man who murdered his own sister and another woman. She suspected there was a deep well of deception surrounding this family.

Ema decided it was time to take the devil by the horns, in a manner of speaking.

17. Blinded by Love

It was late afternoon, and the road lay dappled with swatches of sunlight that filtered through the overhanging branches. Two brick towers marked the entrance to Marysas Plantation. Birds twittered and flew overhead. Insects droned from the tall grass. It appeared a perfect day for a lady to be riding.

Ema led Alegria by the reins as she meandered down the avenue. She wore an emerald green riding habit, with a hat of the same color perched on her head. She stopped and leaned against the thick trunk of a tree, removed a white handkerchief and blotted her forehead. Surreptitiously she scanned around her and saw the main house much further into the property. Much closer, another structure, which she was sure, was the overseer's house had a thin plume of smoke coming from the chimney.

She approached the narrow verandah of the cottage and found it unusual when no one approached her. Ema called out, and still no answer. She mounted the steps and called out again. She then heard a man's voice bidding her to enter.

Inside she found Julian Saturnó sitting in a chair. His tangled black hair hung to his shoulders and his eyes shone with an opaque light. He did not appear surprised to see Ema.

"So you have come for me?" he asked in an apathetic tone.

"I came to speak to you Julian. What binds a creature like you to this family? There is no pleasure here."

"My lust made a slave of me, with a magic that even now I do not understand. But as you know, I am bound by more than one thing." He threw aside the blanket covering his legs, and showed where his ankles, above the large hooves could not move because large manacles bound them together.

"Is this the punishment for coming to Belle Mer?"

"Yes, if I am complacent they are removed, but disobedience is rewarded with this," and his hands swept downward.

Ema saw dry blood caked around the rim of each one.

They both turned their heads when they heard footsteps running up the stairs of the verandah. A slim, teenage girl burst in, panting slightly. Her skin gleamed smooth and dark, and brown eyes blazed in her face. She wore an intricately tied white tignon and large silver earrings.

"Señor Julian, I saw a horse, and I thought you needed me."

Julian's eyes became hooded and secretive. "This is Ines, she looks after me."

Ema thought, "This is a spy who reports on your movements."

She turned to the girl, "Ines, I am a friend of Señor Julian, and I surprised him with a visit. Prepare tea and pastries for us."

The girl glanced uncertainly between Julian and Ema.

Ema asked, "Ines, is anything wrong?"

"No... no," the girl stuttered and trudged off towards the back of the house.

In due course, she reappeared bearing a tray with what Ema had asked for.

Julian met Ema's eyes as she served them tea, and he understood the true purpose of her visit.

Ines inched towards the front door, when he waved her over to his side. "Cariño, please prepare my dinner early, and include an extra serving for Madame, she will be staying. Use whatever is at hand in the kitchen and stay close in case I should have need of you."

The girl nodded reluctantly and turned back towards the kitchen.

Ema turned to Julian and spoke in a language used even before Rome held dominion in the ancient world. "I will free you, but I need you to stay here and pretend you are bound. If you flee, you will make it impossible for me to protect you."

The apathy in the satyr's eyes cleared away, and he nodded.

Ema crouched and took a bar that stretched between each manacle. She glanced up at Julian and whispered, "I am sorry if this causes you further injury, but I cannot help it."

"I will endure it," he stated simply.

She gripped the bar, and her hands became red, where she touched the metal it started to smoke, and with a sudden jerk, she broke the bar. She then grabbed each manacle and broke them apart. Fresh blood started to trickle from the wounds. Ema took the pieces of iron, hid them behind a screen in the corner and draped his legs once again.

In the ancient language, Ema asked him, "What happened?"

"Many years ago, I fell asleep in a place far from here. When I awoke, I found myself in this strange land, and I heard music I could not resist. I left the wilderness and came to a large house. I followed the music to the stables. Inside a handsome man, well dressed spoke to a young girl. Her loveliness ensnared my heart, and her golden hair spun a web of desire as if no other woman existed. I spied on them and overheard their conversation."

"She wanted to leave with him, but he roughly pushed her away and reminded her that his wife waited for him in France. She begged him to take her maidenhead, but he laughed. He said he did not want to stare down the barrel of a pistol in a duel against her father, or one of her uncles. There were many whores he could find pleasure with that would not cost him his life, or his reputation. He told her, 'Obey your parents and marry Girod' and then she screamed invectives at him that made him blanch, and I could see he raised his hand to strike her but stopped himself at the last moment."

"He pushed her to the ground, mounted his horse and rode away. I came to her in the stables, and she gave herself willingly to me. In my blindness I mistook her anger for passion."

"I could not leave this place, and stayed close by in the forest, coming in the evening to be with the golden-haired beauty. Never did I find myself so enraptured with a human woman, and I counted the hours until I could be with her. Then one day I found her crying bitterly in the stables. She wanted none of me, and then for the first time I saw the cruelty in her eyes."

"She told me my child grew inside of her, and her parents in despair agreed to a quick, private marriage with Monsieur Girod before her condition became noticeable. She blamed a simple-minded stable boy as the father, and her parents doubted her words. They only wanted to secure a marriage for her before her reputation lay shredded beyond repair."

Ema then asked him, "Why didn't you leave?"

The man put his head in his hands, and replied, "Because I could not. She enthralled me. But even if I had decided to live without her, I found that if I strayed too far into the woods, I suffered stabbing pains in my gut which ceased when I returned."

"So Noel is your son?"

"Yes, he is, but Monsieur Girod thought she gave birth to a premature child."

"Only later did I realize Assiline's family hid many dark secrets."

From behind where they sat, a silky voice riddled with fury, asked, "Julian, who is this woman? What language are you speaking?"

Ema rose and turned, "My name is Madame Duplessis, I felt unwell while riding my horse. I came here seeking help, and Julian kindly allowed me to stay a few hours until I recovered."

Assiline Girod stared at Ema. Red, angry splotches on her cheekbones stood out on her pale face. Her eyes blazed with barely controlled fury. Her mouth worked back and forth, but she did not speak.

Ema continued, "Madame Girod, I apologize if Julian did not attend to his duties in order to entertain me."

Twilight crept in stealing the last vestiges of the day. In the faltering light, the woman's eyes glittered like shards of glass.

Her voice low and full of menace whispered, "How dare he." From the folds of her skirt she raised a leather quirt and made as if to strike Julian in the face.

The woman cried out as Ema caught her wrist and held it in the air, tightening her grip. Ema pulled the woman against her and caught her by the waist bringing her even closer. Ema leaned in and smelled the woman's hair and the side of her face.

"How unladylike to strike an invalid, but what is much more offensive is that you stink like a dog. When did you last bathe, Madame?"

Assiline Girod screamed in fury and pushed away from Ema who released her. She stumbled backwards, massaging her wrist. Her coiffed hair became undone, and her face contorted. Her breathing became labored and harsh. She started to rend her gown away from her body, with nails that in a moment grew long and curved. Her skin darkened and hair sprouted from every pore of her body, and her face started to change. Bones shifted underneath the skin of her face with a crunch. Her cheekbones widened as her teeth grew long and jagged, filling in a mouth that elongated into a snout. Tufted ears sprouted from between her hair. Her shoulders widened, and her back hunched over creating a grotesque silhouette.

Ines, who arrived with a lighted lamp, let out a thin, high scream and stood there frozen in place, then started babbling, "Loup garou, loup garou!"

Ema whipped around to Julian, "Get her out of here!" She pointed to Ines. Assiline let out a low growl, her eyes glowing like yellow furnaces from hell.

Julian jumped from the invalid chair, and his hooves beat a tattoo on the wooden floor as he grabbed the lamp, took the girl by the waist and hauled her away through the doorway leading towards the back of the house.

Assiline followed them with her eyes and then turned back to Ema. Then she launched herself at the woman, her hands extended to rake her face.

Ema sidestepped her clumsy attack and said, "I accept your challenge."

A dark web of gloominess filled the room, and only a few embers in the fireplace glowed orange. Assiline's howl started low and guttural then rose in a crescendo. Ema recognized her as the creature that stared out from the sugarcane field in Belle Mer. This was the predator that for years terrorized the countryside feasting on human flesh, sometimes for sustenance but many time for the wanton pleasure of the kill.

Ema remembered tales of the Beast of Gévaudan, which terrorized the French countryside in 1764. Could Assiline's family descend from this cursed bloodline? She knew Assiline anticipated she would use one of the two doorways, instead she took the moment and flung herself through a long window. She crashed to the verandah, and in one swift movement jumped the railing. She untied Alegria and slapped her on the rump. The horse sensing the loup garou, galloped off down the road.

Assiline crashed after her, and stood on the verandah, snarling with her tongue lolling out of her mouth. The look of her was obscene, since she appeared as a woman's body covered in fur with the oversized head of a wolf sitting on her shoulders. Only the arms grew longer to allow her to either walk bipedally or run on all four.

Ema took off running into a nearby copse of woods, close behind her she could hear the crash of branches as the loup garou followed her. The trees thinned out, and then beyond in the middle of a clearing stood a small chapel. Surrounded by gravestones it dated back to when France settled the region and Marysas was built.

Ema ran to the narrow entrance of the sanctuary, which allowed space for only a few to sit before the altar. It predated St. Louis Cathedral and visiting clerics celebrated Mass for the family here. She turned and confirmed what she suspected. Assiline could not follow onto consecrated ground, but when human she could enter St. Louis Cathedral, as she did on Ash Wednesday with no sign of discomfort.

The creature screamed in a woman's voice, but then it turned into a howl, and she paced in frustration back and forth at an invisible barrier she could not breach. This proved that Assiline did not serve as an avatar for a dark entity. Her curse came through her bloodline, but Ema could sense the dark sorcery swirling in her wake. Only an experienced practitioner of the dark arts could bind a satyr to a human in this form.

Out of nowhere, a terrific gale moaned, it swept in with a merciless velocity, which she recognized as a portal between dimensions opening. For a few moments, the night sky illuminated with the colors of the aurora borealis. The loup garou threw her head back and howled mournfully, then in the silence that followed not one but several howls answered her. Ema watched Assiline, who stopped making noise, raise her snout and smell the wind. Her stance changed, and Ema could sense her surprise to hear something answer her call. There were no wolves here in this territory, at least none who were wholly animal.

So now, Assiline had to decide if this call signaled a friend or foe, and Ema knew her nature dictated that all were her enemies.

Out of nowhere, a terrific wind lifted Ema up, and she felt pressure grip her as if she swam against a whirlpool. A powerful wind buffeted her body and face from every side. The gale quieted and in its wake came a strong, musky odor. Whatever howled in the distance crept close as the foul scent of a corpse long unburied floated in with a low-lying fog.

The loup garou crouched down. The fur on her back bristled and her ears were laid back. The sound of dry scrabbling came from the brush, as if a large body advanced towards them. She stared at the edge of the woods on the other side of the clearing. Ema then saw eyes as large as dinner plates with an unhealthy greenish white light emanating from them, and narrow vertical red irises.

From behind the clouds, a thin sickle moon silvered the clearing. Assiline issued a nerve-shattering scream, and Ema saw that now she shook like a frightened horse.

From somewhere far off something whined as if in anticipation, but in obedience stayed out of sight. Ema then saw another pair of blazing, gem-like eyes. Another call sounded out, mellowed by distance but grew louder as it came nearer, and then another faint howl re-echoed. Ema's eyes searched the green darkness of the trees since now she knew a pack circled the clearing.

Five shapes stepped out of the woods. They were tall, well over seven feet, and topped by massive wolfish heads. Gray fur covered their muscled bodies. Long arms extended from wide shoulders, and each ended in five fingers with curved claws on the tips. Unlike Assiline, their bodies had no human aspect to them. Except they came forward standing on their hind legs, walking as easily as any human does. They glanced once at Ema, but their attention returned to the loup garou. A leather pouch, suspended by a thong hung around each of their necks.

Assiline now appeared puny next to them, as she slunk to the ground and growled baring her yellow teeth. She sprung forward and away on all four, and as Ema feared, in the house's direction. She dared not risk finding out if they were here only for the loup garou.

DIABOLIQUE
A Sibyl Novella

The creatures did not move until a giant of a beast entered the clearing. His black fur glistened, and there could be no doubt he claimed the title of alpha male. His eyes glittered in the semi-darkness. He stared at the woman as if waiting to see what she intended to do.

Ema understood; if she waited, she lived, but if she ran, she would become prey. She lowered her eyes, as if to refuse his challenge and let them continue after the loup garou. The black one then raised it head into the air and sniffed, the others turned their attention to him.

She felt great danger lay in accepting this choice for it showed weakness on her part. As a hunter herself, she understood that once they finished with the loup garou, they planned to return and kill her. Even if she fled, these swamps were their domain. She had little chance of escape. Could she take the chance? With her diminished powers, battling the loup garou alone was possible, but now the risks so were so much higher. But on the other hand, what if they killed the occupants of Marysas?

The inner voice in her mind reminded in a sibilant whisper, "Only two syllables."

At that moment, Ema picked up her skirts and leaped over one tilting gravestone and then another. She ran fiercely until she reached the treeline. A pandemonium of sound followed her as heavy bodies in full velocity tried to reach her. Once she heard the snap of sharp teeth only inches from her back, and then in a move so quick even they could not comprehend what she did, she turned and plunged straight forward into the onrushing mass of beasts, causing them to halt and scatter.

In her hand, she held a short, metallic staff that glowed blue. This was the only weapon she could muster enough energy to bring to her side. The pack charged her, and she struck, feeling steel bite bone that crunched beneath each stroke. She struck several times and cleared a space around her, waiting for another attack, but none came. One by one, they sank back on their haunches. Their tongues lolled out of wide, gaping jaws as they panted, and eyed the glowing weapon with caution.

She heard a noise behind her, such as a dead leaf and twigs being carried by the wind makes. A faint scrape of claws, a padding of feet and she turned to stare into the red, glaring eyes of the black dogman. He approached and circled around her. She turned always keeping him in sight. Then the five gray ones lifted their heads in unison and issued a long, low wail full of desolation and loneliness. The kill belonged to the leader of the pack. Death stared back at her from the depths of the creature's ruby red eyes.

Ema inhaled deeply, crossed her arms over her chest and said, "*Apis. Regina Apis.*"

In seconds, it felt as if furnace doors opened in the forest. A sirocco of heat blasted through the trees and an orange fiery glow lit up everything. A roar thundered, full of menace and dominion.

Ema stood enfolded by yellow, leathery wings. Above her head towered, the long snout of a beast only seen carved in stone. The creature roared again, and the dogmen scampered off to watch from a distance. They had never seen a dragon, but they knew enough to sense the ones in danger were now them.

The woman reveled in the heat. It did not cause her any harm. Ema stood in front of a beast with gold-colored scales. The fieriness dissipated, and the creature made a purring sound as it nuzzled Ema's hair. Its long tail coiled around her feet in a protective circle.

"Are you still annoyed with me my little Sibyllina?" It questioned her in a soft, raspy voice. "Is fear of death the only reason you say my name?"

Ema leaned back into the soft underbelly of the dragon that cushioned her body. "No Apis, I understand now why you left me behind so long ago. You did it for my good. But I feared that if I called on you again, I'd miss your company too much."

"You have grown strong and independent, but I can see you are still reckless. I can sense these creatures are not evil, but they are predators and hunt out of instinct and control of their territory. They smell your weakness."

Ema nodded in agreement.

The dogmen still looked at the dragon from a distance. The black one came forward, stopped in front of Ema and crouched down. In the mutual respect shared between hunters, she realized that he understood that despite first appearances, she hunted the loup garou as well. They were the ones that interfered with her hunt, and now they were willing to let her continue in the pursuit of her prey.

"You do not need me anymore… for now." The dragon's form started to shimmer and dissipate and her low voice diminished as golden dots like fireflies flew up into the air.

Ema did not wait any longer and ran off into the woods. She didn't know if Assiline could return to human form at will, or if her wolf form held her prisoner until dawn, but either way she could not let her escape. She had only one opportunity, but once she did not act on it, the dogmen as she thought of them now, would take over the hunt.

It proved easy to track Assiline, the fetid odor of a wet dog trailed behind her like a ribbon. Ema found her in a small lean to behind the stables. She could hear the horses inside whinny and knockabout in their stalls in fear as they sensed the loup garou's presence nearby.

Ema heard a step nearby and then Julian stood next to her, stripped of clothes as she saw him that night at Belle Mer.

"So you have run her to ground?" he asked in a quiet voice.

"Not I, she is running from something that she understands that she cannot battle with, much less kill. I have won a reprieve for her but only for a time. Where is Noel?"

"He is in New Orleans."

"Just as well, because he could suffer the same fate as his mother."

"This is my curse. I am bound to her, to protect her even though she is a creature of blood and cruelty. I hate her, but even now I cannot leave her."

"Julian, what is the dark secret that her family hid?"

"They are an old French family, which has suffered from this curse where one of their own has transformed into a wolf, but even when they are mortal they are cruel and unfeeling towards other humans. The family lived in Gévaudan, and one of their own is the one that killed so many in the countryside. The family saw the danger this posed to each one of them. They killed this rogue, and then the family fled to the Louisiana Territory, but they could not outrun the taint on their bloodline. Their young daughter Assiline displayed the characteristics that heralded an ungovernable thirst for killing, just like her uncle."

"They would not kill her?" Ema asked.

Julian shook his head, and continued, "They are vicious but they love their own. She became wild and rebellious, only wanting to consort with unsavory characters. They could not lock her up in a nunnery, so they sought a man eager to marry with lands far from them. Etienne Girod seemed perfect; an older widower, wealthy who lived quite a distance from them. They made their plans, but of course Assiline resisted."

Ema commented drily, "They loved her, but they wanted to distance themselves from her deeds in case she dragged the family down with her. Pragmatists, of course."

The satyr smiled sadly, "They must save the family at all cost and the seeds of my destruction were sown. Only one person claimed Assiline's affection, her nurse, Margot. She asked her help to escape. I believe she is the person who cast this spell on me. She knew Assiline needed protection from her own nature, and who better than a guardian who could not leave, but she also required a husband. Thus she engineered my entry into this place, and her charge's quick marriage to that poor, unsuspecting man. Margot gave Assiline what she needed, not what she wanted. She instructed the family to keep me there with them as an overseer. In due time they sent me to Assiline once her husband fell ill; by then, Noel and his two sisters were born."

Ema eyed Assiline who still slunk in the shadowiness at the back of the building. She snarled and showed her teeth, but she knew what waited for her outside the structure.

Julian continued, "During these years, Assiline pursued prey far afield into the swamps, but a few months ago, something changed and she hunted close to the farms around New Orleans. Noel refuses to see the danger in this."

Ema asked quickly, "Is he like her?"

"No, but he has inherited her savage nature, and seeks to spill blood at every opportunity."

"What has happened to other family members who transformed themselves?"

"Some died in the countryside through unusual accidents, and they never returned from a hunt. Others were imprisoned, but most died at the hands of the family themselves."

"There is no cure for this?"

"No, as they become older, they become more bloodthirsty and transform more often and for longer periods of time. They eventually turn on their own family."

Ema looked into Julian's eyes as she spoke, "Noel has sealed his mother's fate because I doubt he would imprison her."

"No, he would not, and while I would, I cannot let you harm her either."

Ema stared at the satyr, bound by a spell that enslaved him on every level. He was a creature of music and hedonism, who now existed as a pitiful shadow of his true being.

She surprised him by shoving him hard out of her way and entered the lean to brusquely. In a dark corner, the loup garou cowered, and her yellow eyes glimmered as her low snarl filled the silence.

Julian came charging after her, and tackled Ema to the floor, meanwhile shouting to Assiline, "Leave, leave!"

The loup garou hesitated for a moment then dove out a low window. The wooden shutter that covered the opening clacked as the animal leaped outside into the darkness. Ema pushed the satyr off her. He did not realize that she allowed him to bring her to the ground without any resistance. In effect, she allowed him to discharge the strange fealty that bound him to Assiline.

Ema strode outside followed by Julian. In the silence that filled the night, the sound of various, deafening howls sounded close by, followed by a high-pitched woman's moan intermingled with a growl of fury. The sound of rending flesh and bone crunching preceded the smell of fresh-spilled blood.

Julian started to scream in anguish, and then he threw back his head and laughed from deep in his belly. His matted hair grew slick and lustrous, and his pale skin became rosy, his eyes full of mirth and mischievousness.

He turned to Ema. "Return me Sibylline to the place that witch stole me from on that cursed day. This is a dark and bitter land for me, and I am through with my penance."

"As you wish." Ema replied.

The blue bar she held, she tapped once against her thigh and it elongated into a long staff. She drew a large circle in the air, which outlined itself in shifting shades of forest green, and then a door opened. Beyond it lay a lush meadowland surrounded by swaying trees that towered into the air. The scent of pine trees surrounded them. Julian Saturno without a backwards glance ran inside, his long tail flying out behind him like a horse. The circle shrunk and then with a sharp pop disappeared, a few green lights shimmered and then floated to the ground and dissipated.

18. Evil Never Sleeps

Ema found Alegria inside the stable. She saddled her and rode off into the night. She sensed the eyes of the dogmen as they followed her progress through the shadow-dappled road. These creatures killed the harpy. Whether because of dominion over territory or caution of having the balance of their world upset, they did not allow others to hunt what they claimed as theirs. Wisely, they did not want undue attention from the humans that lived on the edges of this unknown land. The struggle for security and survival always won out.

The ride back to New Orleans gave Ema time to think. She wondered what explanation Noel Girod would offer about the disappearance of Julian and his mother. He could not blame the fever as he did with Celeste. For a man like him who suffered a curse in his bloodline, she foresaw they usually brought about their own destruction.

She knew Don Ambrosio left, far but not forever; in due time he would return. This event though could not catch her unprepared.

Another mystery that Ema knew she must solve is the identity of who brought a harpy to this place and bound a satyr to a human. This magic demanded skill and knowledge, and a dangerous disregard for opening portals between dimensions that could only bring disaster if it spilled into this world.

She reached the house on Bourgoine Street in the middle of the night. She went inside after grooming Alegria. She sensed Celeste hovering close by the entrance. Her sister escaped, but her remains still lay in a shallow grave. She could hear her father, but her unhappiness tethered her to this world. Only Celeste had the power to release herself from her regrets.

Once in her bedroom, she stood naked, her full, white breasts gleaming in the oblique darkness. Ema stared at Henry Beasley, and she knew the time had arrived to release him. That night she dreamed of the dragon Apis, and in her sleep, she sighed in contentment as a wound in her heart healed.

In the following days, she conversed with Blanche, and even though her spirit understood the exchange made between her and Ema, she still asked her again if she wished to be her avatar, or find release through a painless death.

With grateful tears, Blanche accepted. As a young woman, she wed an older man in a left-handed marriage, with whom she shared a loving relationship, but he died. Her only child, a son left to France to study and never returned. Only distant relatives living in Mobile were left.

One morning Henry complained to Nicholas of not feeling well, and he even went to see Dr. Destrehan, who knew just by the look of him that his days were numbered. He ordered him to stay at home and leave the running of the business to his partner.

Not too long afterwards, Nicholas Semple arrived to find Henry slumped over his desk. His body felt cold and rigid to the touch. It appeared he died the evening before when he stayed behind to work on accounting ledgers.

Ema dressed in black, with her face veiled by a thin, black mantilla attended the brief funeral and burial at St. Louis Cemetery. After his duel with Noel Girod, Henry had updated his will. Now Nicholas understood that his friend suspected that he escaped death, but only for a short time.

The business went to Nicholas Semple. Madame Duplessis inherited a small fortune, the house on Bourgoine Street and the ownership of the *Venus*. Captain Holbet received the *Syren*. Nicholas and Madame Duplessis would split the proceeds from the sale of his warehouse and home in New York.

Blanche Beaupre moved into the small bedroom in the back of the house and continued in her work as a midwife. When Ema used her as a pocket, she saw a city blossoming on the cusp of a new century. Sin and beauty existed side by side.

During the summer, word reached New Orleans that Captain Juan Sangster died at the hands of his crew onboard the *Lyon* after they mutinied. Fearing retribution, they stole the ship and became pirates.

The summer ended, and those who had left the city in case of contagion, drifted back in to prepare for the winter festivities.

Isabel sat next to Ema after serving her breakfast. She folded her hands on the table. Ema knew this signaled that she wished to discuss something important.

Ema set her fork down and said, "Isabel, speak to me, what worries you so?"

"Someone has been following me for the last two days when I visit the marketplace early in the morning. The first day I could not be sure, but today, I am certain. I came back to the house through a different route so he could not follow."

"Describe this person."

"A monk, but not like the Capuchin at St. Louis. His robes are a different color, and he always has his hood up so I cannot see his face, he is a young man though."

Ema guessed this man sought her whereabouts through her servants.

Two nights later, using Blanche as a pocket she wandered the streets lined with boarding houses and the poorer neighborhoods near the swamp. Before long, they were being followed by someone who stayed at a distance. He hid in inky wedges of gloom every time she stopped at one boarding house or another to inquire if any needed her services.

Outside a corner where two taverns occasionally discharged drunken sailors into the street, Blanche adjusted her basket. Suddenly she turned and stalked towards the man. "Why are you following me?" she asked in a loud voice.

Catching him unaware, he stood there frozen in place.

"Do you need a midwife? Is it for a secret birth? Tell me what you need or stop following me."

"Señora, no I was mistaken." the man replied.

DIABOLIQUE
A Sibyl Novella

Blanche walked closer to him. "Do you think I am blind? You are not the first man to trail after me so I can come and help in the birth of an indiscretion. I know how to keep secrets, otherwise how could I do this for so long? Out with it, what do you want?"

"Nothing, I thought you were someone else."

In a blur, the middle-aged woman with a yellow tignon on her head advanced on the man, grabbed him by the scruff of his collar and placed a carved dagger to his throat.

"What do you want Michael?" Ema's voice and green eyes stared at the startled man's face.

"Lady Sibyl, it is you."

"Answer my question."

He paused, and Ema pressed the point of the knife deeper into his neck.

She knew the Sempiterno Apostasy did not send a messenger just to check on her health. This young man, with brown hair and guileless blue eyes possessed the power of communicating with those who met their end through murder. To send him as an emissary meant danger followed close behind his steps.

In early childhood, he became possessed by a dangerous demon. When freed by exorcism, his village and family shunned him. The Sempiterno Apostasy posing as emissaries from the Vatican took him to a secret place to gauge the effects of the possession. When he celebrated his fifteenth birthday, they inducted him into their order. He displayed the ability to converse with the dead who found no peace. Many secrets became known to this sect from the lips of those silenced by an untimely death.

"Changes, my lady, profound changes are arriving soon. Our enemies in the Vatican, many of them are under the sway of very dark forces. Others are oblivious to this evil, which renders them useless. They implore you to be our eyes and ears. Don Ambrosio is only one of the many dangerous creatures that have been let loose here. Several knew he was a vampire when he traveled to Havana and New Orleans. They orchestrated his exile for only one purpose."

"What purpose is that?"

"He was used to draw you away from Europe. It is you who has been the object of all this subterfuge, not him."

"Treachery, I am well acquainted with it."

He beseeched her with pleading eyes, "Will you help us? There is much work for you here. The dead have told me so."

www.ingramcontent.com/pod-product-compliance
Lightning Source LLC
Chambersburg PA
CBHW030600130626
46552CB00006B/2612